THE SYMBOLIST MOVEMENT
IN LITERATURE

ARTHUR SYMONS, English poet and critic, was born in Wales in 1865. After being privately educated in France and Italy, he embarked on a very productive literary career. Between 1884 and 1886 he edited four of Bernard Quaritch's *Shakespeare Quarto Facsimiles* and from 1888-1889 he edited seven plays in the "Henry Irving" Shakespeare. In 1896 he became editor of the famous magazine, *The Savoy*. Symons' first book of verse, *Days and Nights*, was published in 1889 and was soon followed by further collections of poems, *Silhouettes* (1892), *London Nights* (1896), *Images of Good and Evil* (1899). Among his distinguished volumes of essays are *Studies in Seven Arts* (1906), *The Romantic Movement in English Poetry* (1909). Symons died in 1945.

THE SYMBOLIST MOVEMENT IN LITERATURE was first published in 1899, and revised editions appeared in 1908 and 1919.

THE
SYMBOLIST MOVEMENT
IN LITERATURE

BY
ARTHUR SYMONS
with an Introduction by Richard Ellmann

A Dutton **dep** *Paperback*

NEW YORK
E. P. DUTTON AND CO., INC.

SBN 0-525-47021-2

CONTENTS

INTRODUCTION

Literary movements pass their infancy in revolutionary disaffection, but mature when they achieve a terminology. Late in the nineteenth century the problem was to find the term. In 1899 two new books, one psychological and one literary, fastened on the word *symbolism:* Freud's *Interpretation of Dreams,* which appeared in Vienna in November, and Symons' *The Symbolist Movement in Literature,* published in September in London. Although unlike in method, both recorded the search for a psychic reality which had little to do with exterior reality. Symons' book, like Freud's, gave a name to the preoccupation with modes of half-uttered or half-glimpsed meaning which, as we can see clearly enough now sixty years have passed, was a principal direction in modern thought.

When Symons wrote his book readers in England and the United States were only beginning to be aware of the writers he discussed. The magically operative word "symbolism" brought to a sudden focus the rumors that had drifted slowly into England chiefly from France since 1875, when Mallarmé, his "L'Après-midi d'un Faune" having just roused the French public to derision, paid a visit to Swinburne. Rumors had come also from Ireland since 1887, when W. B. Yeats arrived in London at the age of twenty-two, his mind crowded with occult symbols, eager to defend them with extravagance and cunning. The French reports were a little sinister, of corrupt lives, enigmatic and probably immoral works, and those from Ireland were at once crepuscular and provincial, so that it remained easy, until Arthur Symons' book appeared, to ignore them. The official view, heard commonly in France and England after the death of Hugo in

1885 and then of Browning and Tennyson a few years later, was that poetry was dead. This was the verdict of René Doumic in the august *Revue des Deux Mondes* in 1894. Symons suddenly joined issue with this attitude of resignation. He found poetry decidedly alive and on its way to embracing, more and more completely, this new-old doctrine of symbolism. Writers who had been hesitating towards a new conception of literature—impersonal where the romantics had been personal, reticent where the romantics had been indiscreet, esoteric where the romantics had been popular—saw their intentions suddenly clarified into the philosophy of a school. Unlike the Pre-Raphaelites, who had been skimpy of theory, the symbolists were prodigal of it, in their gnomic way.

It was no doubt a little embarrassing to Symons that he had to represent as his avant-garde a group of writers who were anything but young. Of those he discusses, Nerval was not so much symbolism's father as its grandfather (its father was Baudelaire), having died in 1855; five of Symons' other examples (Laforgue, Villiers, Rimbaud, Verlaine, and Mallarmé) had died between 1887 and 1898. The only two living exponents of symbolism with whom he dealt were Maeterlinck and Huysmans, neither of them fledglings. But the lives and works of all these writers retained enough tumult to satisfy the demand for strangeness and novelty, and Symons turned the scandal that hung over them into a glamor previously reserved for the English romantic poets.

Before Symons the main middleman between English and French culture was George Moore. Moore went to Paris in the late 1870's and met Villiers de l'Isle-Adam, Mallarmé, Verlaine, and others. Many of these, as well as Rimbaud, are mentioned in his *Confessions of a Young Man* (1888). It was Moore who introduced Huysmans' *À Rebours* (1884) before Wilde described the book in *The Picture of Dorian Gray* (1890). As he was inclined to boast, Moore also wrote the first articles in English on Rimbaud, Laforgue, and Verlaine, collecting them in 1891 in his *Impressions and Opinions*. Edmund Gosse was to follow him by writing the first English critical essay on Mallarmé in his *Questions at Issue,* published in 1893. This was the year, too, when Verlaine came to England in November to lecture at Oxford; a little later, in March, 1894, Mallarmé also lectured at Oxford and at Cambridge. The same month Villiers' *Axël* was produced in Paris for the first time, and in the audience was W. B. Yeats, who was so moved that he entered it thereafter among his "sacred books." Translations of the symbolist writers began to appear in the middle 'nineties, and when Verlaine died in 1896 and Mallarmé two years later, Symons must have recognized his call to systematize what Moore and others had only touched with the ends of their fingers.

That it should have been Symons who wrote the first book in English expressly devoted to the French symbolists was not strange. A Cornishman born in Wales, who prided himself on not being English, he came to London while still young and set himself promptly to the task of showing that the English, rather than himself, were the provincials. He sought out sensations, not to be overwhelmed by them, but to become their connoisseur. His early volumes of verse suggest an almost frantic search for deeper emotions than he was able to attain, along with a sophisticated curiosity about all feelings. It was during this period, as he said later, that he took hashish fairly regularly, no doubt tasting his way towards new thresholds. All the arts attracted him: he played the piano, went to concerts, studied Whistler and the French Impressionists, attended music halls, ballets, plays. His personal life was apparently a succession of love affairs of brief duration, often with ballet dancers and circus performers. Once he surprised a friend by confiding to him, "I was never in love with a serpent-charmer before." Books, especially foreign books, attracted him as much as poised women; he responded to them all urbanely. His critical articles, witty, informed, sensible, and grace-

ful, as befitted a friend and admirer of Pater, and somewhat lacking in emphasis too, were soon appearing in the
Athenaeum and elsewhere. When he became editor
of the *Savoy* in 1896, at the age of thirty-one, he occupied
a position in England as the principal interpreter of con-
tinental writers, which was like that of Valery Larbaud
in Paris in 1920.

His interest in France was consolidated by a trip to
Paris in 1889 with Havelock Ellis as his companion.
They visited Mallarmé on a Tuesday evening, and met
also Huysmans, Maeterlinck, and other prominent
writers. Villiers, whom they had hoped to see, disobliged
them by dying shortly before their arrival; but Symons
wrote an obituary article on him for Oscar Wilde's
magazine, the *Woman's World*. This was not only the
first article in English on Villiers but also the first of
Symons' studies of the symbolists. The visit apparently
confirmed his ambition for an international acquaintance,
and the next year and regularly thereafter he returned
to Paris. In 1890 Charles Morice introduced Symons to
Verlaine, and Verlaine's trip to England in 1893 came
about largely as a result of Symons' arrangements, which
Verlaine rewarded with a delightful poem. For a few
days Verlaine was Symons' guest at Fountain Court in
the Temple; they translated some of each other's works,
and Symons presented his friend to most of the London
literary men.

What Symons lacked as a critic was the ability to
generalize (his remarks are better than his conclusions),
yet paradoxically the importance of his book on symbolism was its ruling generalization. That the movement
should be called "symbolist" was a point still blurred in
France, and Symons did not at first acknowledge it. In
an essay of 1893 he preferred, while dismissing the question of the name as of no great consequence, to use the
term "decadent" rather than "symbolist." He was in
tune, then, with Gosse and Wilde, who regarded symbolism as a fascinating disease, and not much at odds

with Moore, who scoffed at it as just "saying the opposite of what you mean." It was W. B. Yeats who seems to have persuaded Symons that the season was not autumn but spring, and encouraged him to see symbolism as the soul's heroic recovery of authority over the body and the material world.

Symons' acquaintance with Yeats began about 1891 in the Rhymers' Club, a group of poets who met at the Cheshire Cheese. The club took its name partly to shun pomposity, but also to avoid commitment to anything but the writing of perfect songs. Symons and Yeats seem to have come together in part because Symons was as eager to hear general statements about literature as Yeats was to impart them. Symons, predisposed by his respect for the French to subscribe to large ideas, sometimes adapted for the other Rhymers what he had heard in France, and said, "We are concerned with nothing but impressions." But the others, poets like Lionel Johnson and Ernest Dowson, gave him no encouragement. They checked Yeats's theories, which were more tendentious, with even greater curtness. As a result Symons and Yeats talked a good deal to each other. Late in 1895 Yeats moved into rooms that connected with Symons' in Fountain Court, and for over a year they shared food, friends, and ideas.

It seems reasonably clear that Yeats's mind was the dominant one in the friendship. He had evolved already a symbology which, while backed by occult ideas, did not depend upon them, and he was endeavoring to give the new Irish literary movement a symbolic direction. He had published with Edwin Ellis a three-volume edition of Blake that flaunted Blake's symbolism and attempted to explain it; and in his essays from 1893 on the word "symbolical," as magical as "Celtic," was a battlecry which he allowed nothing except perhaps his heavily rhythmed prose to mute. Symons followed him to Blake, to symbolic theory, and to mysticism.

But Symons was also useful to Yeats who, with his poor French, would hardly have dared to speak of the symbolists in France with any confidence if his friend had not helped him to read them. He was pleased to discover how far French masters had already gone on the way he had marked out for himself. Symons talked a good deal about them, and read out to Yeats his translations of Mallarmé and Verlaine. The two attended together a performance of Jarry's *Ubu Roi,* Symons interpreting. In response to this prodding Yeats began to list Mallarmé and Verlaine, as well as Villiers and Maeterlinck, as participants in a movement he traced back to the Pre-Raphaelites in England.

There is a good instance of the collaboration of the two friends in a preface which Symons wrote in 1896 for a second edition of his book of verse, *Silhouettes.* He and Yeats were traveling together in Ireland, and the preface was completed at Rosses Point, Sligo, where Yeats had spent much of his childhood. In the preface Symons shifts from his own favorite word "impressions" to Yeats's favorite, "moods," and defends his poems as the depiction of moods for their own sake. This is good and bad Yeats, for to Yeats the doctrine of moods was sanctioned by the occult theory that the moods are eternal and impersonal states of mind into which poems might occasionally infiltrate. For Symons the justification was that anything ever experienced by a human being is worth writing about. Symons' theory was too disconnected for Yeats, who reproved him later for the theory of *isolated* lyrical moments; and in his later writings, though Yeats discussed Symons with affection, he could not forbear to indicate that his friend's mind was, by his lights, too fragmentary.

Mostly under Yeats's influence, then, as it seems, Symons decided to publish a book on the French writers as members of a movement. Yeats's phrase, "the symbolical movement," was too general; by calling it "the symbolist movement" Symons made it more special, topical, and doctrinaire. With this theme he hoped to establish the outlines of an esthetic system that could bind the separate essays he had published between 1895 and 1898 on Huysmans, Mallarmé, Nerval, Rimbaud, Villiers, Verlaine, and Maeterlinck. He retouched them, added an essay on Laforgue, then wrote an introduction and conclusion to embody the new insight Yeats had helped him to reach, the perception of a singleness of purpose among these disparate talents.

Symons does, it is true, use the term "symbolism" rather loosely. In the essays on Nerval and Villiers symbolism is primarily the perception of a reality which is opposite to the world of appearance; in the essays on Mallarmé and Maeterlinck this reality is not opposed to appearance, but is just barely over its borders; with Rimbaud and Verlaine, on the other hand, symbolism is the perception of the world of appearance with a visionary intensity; with Huysmans symbolism is the understanding of the organic unity of the world of appearance. Symons includes among the symbolists those who reject the world, those who accept it so totally as to see it with new eyes, and those who regard it under the aspect of eternity. He is less adroit than Yeats in manipulating the contrasting values of the words "appearance" and "reality," and understands vaguely, if at all, the Yeatsian view of the interpenetration of the two worlds. Yet a stricter definition of terms would have raised problems of application to particular authors that still perplex the literary historian.

In our day, when critical prose has become the straightest line between two points, some of Symons' subtleties in his book may be overlooked. His style is made up of delicacies and insinuations. Considering as he does that symbolist literature is "a sacred ritual," he treats each of his authors as a renunciant, who gives up contentment for the sake of his soul and art. Although occasionally Symons supplies a date, his portraits are almost timeless, and could be set in his book of fictitious *Spiritual Adventures* without looking very different from the characters there. These men are so strange that it seems almost problematical that they lived at all. Symons discovers them, and they discover him, finally turning, or almost turning, into aspects of his own mind struggling for expression, then dying out. Their lives seem to pass in a dream; their odd or immoral behavior simply makes the dream richer. At the end, so personal is the book, so intricate the bond of writer and reader, we are willing to concede Symons' extraordinary conclusion, that these symbolist writers may help to reconcile us to death.

The Symbolist Movement in Literature became Symons' most popular book, and in 1908 he published a second edition with a few minor changes, chiefly to bring the essay on Huysmans, who had died in 1907, up to date. Then Symons experienced the mental breakdown and madness which he has described in his *Confessions* with many references to the corresponding madness of Gérard de Nerval. He recovered his faculties in two years, but not his force. The next edition of *The Symbolist Movement,* in 1919, shows a curious indifference to the book's earlier rationale; he leaves out the dedication to Yeats and, while retaining the title, interpolates a series of essays on nineteenth-century French writers most of whom, as he had said explicitly in the "Introduction," were not symbolists. An exception was Baudelaire, included at last, though Symons was to be chided afterwards by T. S. Eliot for not appreciating Baudelaire properly. Finally, for his *Collected Works* in 1924 Symons swelled the book further by combining with it a series of essays on English writers; he now gave it the unexceptionable but nondescript title, *Studies in Two Literatures.*

It has seemed advisable to combat Symons' own dilution of his book by printing the 1908 text, substantially the same as that of 1899, in its original order. The essays interpolated in 1919, some of them good but mostly irrelevant to symbolism, have been moved to the second part of this new edition. So it is possible to recover the excitement of the book as it was felt by Eliot, for example, who said of it in 1930, "I myself owe Mr. Symons a great debt: but for having read his book I should not, in the year 1908, have heard of Laforgue or Rimbaud; I should probably not have begun to read Verlaine; and but for reading Verlaine, I should not have heard of Corbière."

To read the book through Eliot's eyes is to renew his excitement. For him the most notable essay was apparently that on Laforgue, whose gentlemanly despair he was to incorporate in "Prufrock." Of the four poems of Laforgue that Symons quotes, Eliot made free adaptations of two; one of these, "Conversation Galante," earned a place in his *Collected Poems*. Eliot was probably also impressed by what Symons had to say, in the essays on Nerval and Laforgue, of the method of setting familiar and apparently alien things together, of detecting the hidden links of distant and divergent things. He caught up this hint in his essay on "The Metaphysical Poets," where he finds a surprising resemblance between Laforgue and Donne.

Symons' success with his essays and book on French literature had their effect upon other young writers. Both John Synge and James Joyce followed him to Paris and tried unsuccessfully to become equally famous transmitters of foreign culture. Synge gave it up and went to Aran; Joyce gave it up and went at last to Trieste. After Symons the need in English was not for critics but for makers, and they became their own symbolists. Among Symons' later contributions to the movement, not the least was his benevolent assistance to Joyce in finding him a publisher for *Chamber Music*. That book, Joyce's first, belonged to Symons' own type of symbolistic verse, as George Moore perceived.

There are moments in literature when the important thing is to suspect, to hint, to leap, and there are moments when the important thing is to conclude, to bring together, to bind. Symons found a moment of the second sort, and, with his marvellous adaptability, took possession of it. The result was to import into modern literature the word "symbol" much as Wordsworth, a hundred years before, had pressed upon romantic literature the word "nature." Since 1899 the French symbolists have steadily affected even writers who have not read them, and for this fortunate exchange Arthur Symons, who was among those who read them first, was chiefly responsible.

RICHARD ELLMANN

Northwestern University
1958

BIBLIOGRAPHICAL NOTE

The reader who wishes to pursue the subject of symbolism will find the following books useful: for the ideology of French symbolism, A. G. Lehmann, *The Symbolist Esthetic in France* (1950); for its detailed history and a bibliography of French works about it, Kenneth Cornell, *The Symbolist Movement* (1951); for symbolism in the twentieth century, Edmund Wilson, *Axel's Castle* (1931), C. M. Bowra, *The Heritage of Symbolism* (1943), W. Y. Tindall, *The Literary Symbol* (1957), and Edwin Honig, *Dark Conceit: The Making of Allegory* (1959); for symbolism in American literature, Charles Feidelson, Jr., *Symbolism and American Literature* (1953), and Harry Levin, *The Power of Blackness* (1958). An examination of the philosophical implications of symbolism can be found in the writings of Ernst Cassirer and, on a more accessible level, of Susanne Langer. For Arthur Symons' critical theories see Ruth Z. Temple, *The Critic's Alchemy* (1953), and Frank Kermode, *Romantic Image* (1957).

R. E.

TO W. B. YEATS

May I dedicate to you this book on the Symbolist movement in literature, both as an expression of a deep personal friendship and because you, more than any one else, will sympathise with what I say in it, being yourself the chief representative of that movement in our country? France is the country of movements, and it is naturally in France that I have studied the development of a principle which is spreading throughout other countries, perhaps not less effectually, if with less definite outlines. Your own Irish literary movement is one of its expressions; your own poetry and A. E.'s poetry belong to it in the most intimate sense. In Germany it seems to be permeating the whole of literature, its spirit is that which is deepest in Ibsen, it has absorbed the one new force in Italy, Gabriele d'Annunzio. I am told of a group of Symbolists in Russian literature, there is another in Dutch literature, in Portugal it has a little school of its own under Eugenio de Castro; I even saw some faint strivings that way in Spain, and the aged Spanish poet Campoamor has always fought on behalf of a "transcendental" art in which we should recognise much of what is most essential in the doctrine of Symbolism. How often have you and I discussed all these questions, rarely arguing about them, for we rarely had an essential difference of opinion, but bringing them more and more clearly into light, turning our instincts into logic, digging until we reached the bases of our convictions. And all the while we were working as well as thinking out a philosophy of art; you, at all events, creating beautiful things, as beautiful, it seems to me, as anything that is being done in our time.

And we talked of other things besides art, and there are other sympathies, besides purely artistic ones, between us. I speak often in this book of Mysticism, and that I, of all people, should venture to speak, not quite as an outsider, of such things, will probably be a surprise to many. It will be no surprise to you, for you have seen me gradually finding my way, uncertainly but inevitably, in that direction which has always been to you your natural direction. Still, as I am, so meshed about with the variable and too clinging appearances of things, so weak before the delightfulness of earthly circumstance, I hesitate sometimes in saying what I have in my mind, lest I should seem to be saying more than I have any personal right to say. But what, after all, is one's personal right? How insignificant a matter to any one but oneself, a matter how deliberately to be disregarded in that surely impersonal utterance which comes to one in one's most intimate thinking about beauty and truth and the deeper issues of things!

It is almost worth writing a book to have one perfectly sympathetic reader, who will understand everything that one has said, and more than one has said, who will think one's own thought whenever one has said exactly the right thing, who will complete what is imperfect in reading it, and be too generous to think that it is imperfect. I feel that I shall have that reader in you; so here is my book in token of that assurance.

ARTHUR SYMONS

London, *June* 1899

THE SYMBOLIST MOVEMENT
IN LITERATURE

INTRODUCTION

"It is in and through Symbols that man, consciously or un-consciously, lives, works, and has his being: those ages, moreover, are accounted the noblest which can the best recognise symbolical worth, and prize it highest."

CARLYLE.

WITHOUT symbolism there can be no literature; indeed, not even language. What are words themselves but symbols, almost as arbitrary as the letters which compose them, mere sounds of the voice to which we have agreed to give certain significations, as we have agreed to translate these sounds by those combinations of letters? Symbolism began with the first words uttered by the first man, as he named every living thing; or before them, in heaven, when God named the world into being. And we see, in these beginnings, precisely what Symbolism in literature really is: a form of expression, at the best but approximate, essentially but arbitrary, until it has ob-tained the force of a convention, for an unseen reality apprehended by the consciousness. It is sometimes per-mitted to us to hope that our convention is indeed the reflection rather than merely the sign of that unseen reality. We have done much if we have found a recognisable sign.

"A symbol," says Comte Goblet d'Alviella, in his book on *The Migration of Symbols,* "might be defined as a representation which does not aim at being a repro-duction." Originally, as he points out, used by the Greeks to denote "the two halves of the tablet they divided between themselves as a pledge of hospitality,"

1

it came to be used of every sign, formula, or rite by which those initiated in any mystery made themselves secretly known to one another. Gradually the word extended its meaning, until it came to denote every conventional representation of idea by form, of the unseen by the visible. "In a Symbol," says Carlyle, "there is concealment and yet revelation: hence therefore, by Silence and by Speech acting together, comes a double significance." And, in that fine chapter of *Sartor Resartus,* he goes further, vindicating for the word its full value: "In the Symbol proper, what we can call a Symbol, there is ever, more or less distinctly and directly, some embodiment and revelation of the Infinite; the Infinite is made to blend itself with the Finite, to stand visible, and as it were, attainable there."

It is in such a sense as this that the word Symbolism has been used to describe a movement which, during the last generation, has profoundly influenced the course of French literature. All such words, used of anything so living, variable, and irresponsible as literature, are, as symbols themselves must so often be, mere compromises, mere indications. Symbolism, as seen in the writers of our day, would have no value if it were not seen also, under one disguise or another, in every great imaginative writer. What distinguishes the Symbolism of our day from the Symbolism of the past is that it has now become conscious of itself, in a sense in which it was unconscious even in Gérard de Nerval, to whom I trace the particular origin of the literature which I call Symbolist. The forces which mould the thought of men change, or men's resistance to them slackens; with the change of men's thought comes a change of literature, alike in its inmost essence and in its outward form: after the world has starved its soul long enough in the contemplation and the re-arrangement of material things, comes the turn of the soul; and with it comes the literature of which I write in this volume, a literature in which the visible world is no longer a reality, and the unseen world no longer a dream.

The great epoch in French literature which preceded this epoch was that of the offshoot of Romanticism which produced Baudelaire, Flaubert, the Goncourts, Taine, Zola, Leconte de Lisle. Taine was the philosopher both of what had gone before him and of what came immediately after; so that he seems to explain at once Flaubert and Zola. It was the age of Science, the age of material things; and words, with that facile elasticity which there is in them, did miracles in the exact representation of everything that visibly existed, exactly as it existed. Even Baudelaire, in whom the spirit is always an uneasy guest at the orgy of life, had a certain theory of Realism which tortures many of his poems into strange, metallic shapes, and fills them with imitative odours, and disturbs them with a too deliberate rhetoric of the flesh. Flaubert, the one impeccable novelist who has ever lived, was resolute to be the novelist of a world in which art, formal art, was the only escape from the burden of reality, and in which the soul was of use mainly as the agent of fine literature. The Goncourts caught at Impressionism to render the fugitive aspects of a world which existed only as a thing of flat spaces, and angles, and coloured movement, in which sun and shadow were the artists; as moods, no less flitting, were the artists of the merely receptive consciousness of men and women. Zola has tried to build in brick and mortar inside the covers of a book; he is quite sure that the soul is a nervous fluid, which he is quite sure some man of science is about to catch for us, as a man of science has bottled the air, a pretty, blue liquid. Leconte de Lisle turned the world to stone, but saw, beyond the world, only a pause from misery in a Nirvana never subtilised to the Eastern ecstasy. And, with all these writers, form aimed above all things at being precise, at saying rather than suggesting, at saying what they had to say so completely that nothing remained over, which it might be the business of the reader to divine. And so they have expressed, finally, a certain aspect of the world; and some of them have carried style to a point beyond which the style that says, rather than suggests, cannot go. The whole of that movement comes to a splendid funeral in Heredia's sonnets, in which the literature of form says its last word, and dies.

Meanwhile, something which is vaguely called Decadence had come into being. That name, rarely used with any precise meaning, was usually either hurled as a reproach or hurled back as a defiance. It pleased some young men in various countries to call themselves Decadents, with all the thrill of unsatisfied virtue masquerading as uncomprehended vice. As a matter of fact, the term is in its place only when applied to style; to that ingenious deformation of the language, in Mallarmé, for instance, which can be compared with what we are accustomed to call the Greek and Latin of the Decadence. No doubt perversity of form and perversity of matter are often found together, and, among the lesser men especially, experiment was carried far, not only in the direction of style. But a movement which in this sense might be called Decadent could but have been a straying aside from the main road of literature. Nothing, not even conventional virtue, is so provincial as conventional vice; and the desire to "bewilder the middle classes" is itself middle-class. The interlude, half a mock-interlude, of Decadence, diverted the attention of the critics while something more serious was in preparation. That something more serious has crystallised, for the time, under the form of Symbolism, in which art returns to the one pathway, leading through beautiful things to the eternal beauty.

In most of the writers whom I have dealt with as summing up in themselves all that is best in Symbolism, it will be noticed that the form is very carefully elaborated, and seems to count for at least as much as in those writers of whose over-possession by form I have complained. Here, however, all this elaboration comes from a very different motive, and leads to other ends. There is such a thing as perfecting form that form may be annihilated. All the art of Verlaine is in bringing verse to a bird's song, the art of Mallarmé in bringing verse to the song of an orchestra. In Villiers de l'Isle-Adam drama becomes an embodiment of spiritual forces, in Maeterlinck not even their embodiment, but the remote sound of their voices. It is all an attempt to spiritualise literature, to evade the old bondage of rhetoric, the old bondage of exteriority. Description is banished that beautiful things may be evoked, magically; the regular beat of verse is broken in order that words may fly, upon subtler wings. Mystery is no longer feared, as the great mystery in whose midst we are islanded was feared by those to whom that unknown sea was only a great void. We are coming closer to nature, as we seem to shrink from it with something of horror, disdaining to catalogue the trees of the forest. And as we brush aside the accidents of daily life, in which men and women imagine that they are alone touching reality, we come closer to humanity, to everything in humanity that may have begun before the world and may outlast it.

Here, then, in this revolt against exteriority, against rhetoric, against a materialistic tradition; in this endeavour to disengage the ultimate essence, the soul, of whatever exists and can be realised by the consciousness; in this dutiful waiting upon every symbol by which the soul of things can be made visible; literature, bowed down by so many burdens, may at last attain liberty, and its authentic speech. In attaining this liberty, it accepts a heavier burden; for in speaking to us so intimately, so solemnly, as only religion had hitherto spoken to us, it becomes itself a kind of religion, with all the duties and responsibilities of the sacred ritual.

GÉRARD DE NERVAL

I

THIS is the problem of one who lost the whole world and gained his own soul.

"I like to arrange my life as if it were a novel," wrote Gérard de Nerval, and, indeed, it is somewhat difficult to disentangle the precise facts of an existence which was never quite conscious where began and where ended that "overflowing of dreams into real life," of which he speaks. "I do not ask of God," he said, "that he should change anything in events themselves, but that he should change me in regard to things, so that I might have the power to create my own universe about me, to govern my dreams, instead of enduring them." The prayer was not granted, in its entirety; and the tragedy of his life lay in the vain endeavour to hold back the irresistible empire of the unseen, which it was the joy of his life to summon about him. Briefly, we know that Gérard Labrunie (the name de Nerval was taken from a little piece of property, worth some 1500 francs, which he liked to imagine had always been in the possession of his family) was born at Paris, May 22, 1808. His father was surgeon-major; his mother died before he was old enough to remember her, following the *Grande Armée* on the Russian campaign; and Gérard was brought up, largely under the care of a studious and erratic uncle, in a little village called Montagny, near Ermenonville. He was a precocious schoolboy, and by the age of eighteen had published six little collections of verses. It was during one of his holidays that he saw, for the first and last time, the young girl whom he calls Adrienne, and whom, under many names, he loved to the end of his life. One evening she had come from the château to dance with the young peasant girls on the grass. She had danced with Gérard, he had kissed her cheek, he had crowned her hair with laurels, he had heard her sing an old song telling of the sorrows of a princess whom her father had shut in a tower because she had loved. To Gérard it seemed that already he remembered her, and certainly he was never to forget her. Afterwards, he heard that Adrienne had taken the veil; then, that she was dead. To one who had realised that it is "we, the living, who walk in a world of phantoms," death could not exclude hope; and when, many years later, he fell seriously and fantastically in love with a little actress called Jenny Colon, it was because he seemed to have found, in that blonde and very human person, the re-incarnation of the blonde Adrienne.

Meanwhile Gérard was living in Paris, among his friends the Romantics, writing and living in an equally desultory fashion. *Le bon Gérard* was the best loved, and, in his time, not the least famous, of the company. He led, by choice, now in Paris, now across Europe, the life of a vagabond, and more persistently than others of his friends who were driven to it by need. At that time, when it was the aim of every one to be as eccentric as possible, the eccentricities of Gérard's life and thought seemed, on the whole, less noticeable than those of many really quite normal persons. But with Gérard there was no pose; and when, one day, he was found in the Palais-Royal, leading a lobster at the end of a blue ribbon (because, he said, it does not bark, and knows the secrets of the sea), the visionary had simply lost control of his visions, and had to be sent to Dr. Blanche's asylum at Montmartre. He entered March 21, 1841, and came out, apparently well again, on the 21st of November. It would seem that this first access of madness was, to some extent, the consequence of the final rupture with Jenny

Colon; on June 5, 1842, she died, and it was partly in order to put as many leagues of the earth as possible between him and that memory that Gérard set out, at the end of 1842, for the East. It was also in order to prove to the world, by his consciousness of external things, that he had recovered his reason. While he was in Syria, he once more fell in love with a new incarnation of Adrienne, a young Druse, Saléma, the daughter of a Sheikh of Lebanon; and it seems to have been almost by accident that he did not marry her. He returned to Paris at the end of 1843 or the beginning of 1844, and for the next few years he lived mostly in Paris, writing charming, graceful, remarkably sane articles and books, and wandering about the streets, by day and night, in a perpetual dream, from which, now and again, he was somewhat rudely awakened. When, in the spring of 1853, he went to see Heine, for whom he was doing an admirable prose translation of his poems, and told him he had come to return the money he had received in advance, because the times were accomplished, and the end of the world, announced by the Apocalypse, was at hand, Heine sent for a cab, and Gérard found himself at Dr. Dubois' asylum, where he remained two months. It was on coming out of the asylum that he wrote *Sylvie,* a delightful idyl, chiefly autobiographical, one of his three actual achievements. On August 27, 1853, he had to be taken to Dr. Blanche's asylum at Passy, where he remained till May 27, 1854. Thither, after a month or two spent in Germany, he returned on August 8, and on October 19 he came out for the last time, manifestly uncured. He was now engaged on the narrative of his own madness, and the first part of *Le Rêve et la Vie* appeared in the *Revue de Paris* of January 1, 1855. On the 20th he came into the office of the review, and showed Gautier and Maxime du Camp an apron-string which he was carrying in his pocket. "It is the girdle," he said, "that Madame de Maintenon wore when she had *Esther* performed at Saint-Cyr." On the 24th he wrote to a friend:

"Come and prove my identity at the police-station of the Châtelet." The night before he had been working at his manuscript in a pot-house of Les Halles, and had been arrested as a vagabond. He was used to such little mis-adventures, but he complained of the difficulty of writing. "I set off after an idea," he said, "and lose myself; I am hours in finding my way back. Do you know I can scarcely write twenty lines a day, the darkness comes about me so close!" He took out the apron-string. "It is the garter of the Queen of Sheba," he said. The snow was freezing on the ground, and on the night of the 25th, at three in the morning, the landlord of a "penny doss" in the Rue de la Vieille-Lanterne, a filthy alley lying between the quays and the Rue de Rivoli, heard some one knocking at the door, but did not open, on account of the cold. At dawn, the body of Gérard de Nerval was found hanging by the apron-string to a bar of the window.

It is not necessary to exaggerate the importance of the half-dozen volumes which make up the works of Gérard de Nerval. He was not a great writer; he had moments of greatness; and it is the particular quality of these moments which is of interest for us. There is the en-tertaining, but not more than entertaining, *Voyage en Orient;* there is the estimable translation of *Faust,* and the admirable versions from Heine; there are the volumes of short stories and sketches, of which even *Les Illuminés,* in spite of the promise of its title, is little more than an agreeable compilation. But there remain three composi-tions: the sonnets, *Le Rêve et la Vie,* and *Sylvie;* of which *Sylvie* is the most objectively achieved, a wandering idyl, full of pastoral delight, and containing some folk-songs of Valois, two of which have been translated by Rossetti; *Le Rêve et la Vie* being the most intensely personal, a narrative of madness, unique as madness itself; and the sonnets, a kind of miracle, which may be held to have created something at least of the method of the later Symbolists. These three compositions, in which alone

Gérard is his finest self, all belong to the periods when he was, in the eyes of the world, actually mad. The sonnets belong to two of these periods, *Le Rêve et la Vie* to the last; *Sylvie* was written in the short interval between the two attacks in the early part of 1853. We have thus the case of a writer, graceful and elegant when he is sane, but only inspired, only really wise, passionate, collected, only really master of himself, when he is insane. It may be worth looking at a few of the points which so suggestive a problem presents to us.

II

Gerard de Nerval lived the transfigured inner life of the dreamer. "I was very tired of life!" he says. And like so many dreamers, who have all the luminous darkness of the universe in their brains, he found his most precious and uninterrupted solitude in the crowded and more sordid streets of great cities. He who had loved the Queen of Sheba, and seen the seven Elohims dividing the world, could find nothing more tolerable in mortal conditions, when he was truly aware of them, than the company of the meanest of mankind, in whom poverty and vice, and the hard pressure of civilisation, still leave some of the original vivacity of the human comedy. The real world seeming to be always so far from him, and a sort of terror of the gulfs holding him, in spite of himself, to its flying skirts, he found something at all events realisable, concrete, in these drinkers of Les Halles, these vagabonds of the Place du Carrousel, among whom he so often sought refuge. It was literally, in part, a refuge. During the day he could sleep, but night wakened him, and that restlessness, which the night draws out in those who are really under lunar influences, set his feet wandering, if only in order that his mind might wander the less. The sun, as he mentions, never appears in dreams; but, with the approach of night, is not every one a little

readier to believe in the mystery lurking behind the
world?

Crains, dans le mur aveugle, un regard qui t'épie!

he writes in one of his great sonnets; and that fear of
the invisible watchfulness of nature was never absent
from him. It is one of the terrors of human existence that
we may be led at once to seek and to shun solitude; unable to bear the mortal pressure of its embrace, unable
to endure the nostalgia of its absence. "I think man's
happiest when he forgets himself," says an Elizabethan
dramatist; and, with Gérard, there was Adrienne to
forget, and Jenny Colon the actress, and the Queen of
Sheba. But to have drunk of the cup of dreams is to
have drunk of the cup of eternal memory. The past, and,
as it seemed to him, the future were continually with
him; only the present fled continually from under his
feet. It was only by the effort of this contact with people
who lived so sincerely in the day, the minute, that he
could find even a temporary foothold. With them, at
least, he could hold back all the stars, and the darkness
beyond them, and the interminable approach and disappearance of all the ages, if only for the space between
tavern and tavern, where he could open his eyes on so
frank an abandonment to the common drunkenness of
most people in this world, here for once really living the
symbolic intoxication of their ignorance.

Like so many dreamers of illimitable dreams, it was
the fate of Gérard to incarnate his ideal in the person of
an actress. The fatal transfiguration of the footlights,
in which reality and the artificial change places with
so fantastic a regularity, has drawn many moths into its
flame, and will draw more, as long as men persist in
demanding illusion of what is real, and reality in what
is illusion. The Jenny Colons of the world are very
simple, very real, if one will but refrain from assuming
them to be a mystery. But it is the penalty of all imagi-

native lovers to create for themselves the veil which hides
from them the features of the beloved. It is their privi-
lege, for it is incomparably more entrancing to fancy
oneself in love with Isis than to know that one is in
love with Manon Lescaut. The picture of Gérard, after
many hesitations, revealing to the astonished Jenny that
she is the incarnation of another, the shadow of a dream,
that she has been Adrienne and is about to be the
Queen of Sheba; her very human little cry of pure
incomprehension, *Mais vous ne m'aimez pas!* and her
prompt refuge in the arms of the *jeune premier ridé,* if
it were not of the acutest pathos, would certainly be of
the most quintessential comedy. For Gérard, so sharp an
awakening was but like the passage from one state to
another, across that little bridge of one step which lies
between heaven and hell, to which he was so used in his
dreams. It gave permanency to the trivial, crystallising
it, in another than Stendhal's sense; and when death
came, changing mere human memory into the terms of
eternity, the darkness of the spiritual world was lit with
a new star, which was henceforth the wandering, desolate
guide of so many visions. The tragic figure of Aurélia,
which comes and goes through all the labyrinths of dream,
is now seen always "as if lit up by a lightning-flash, pale
and dying, hurried away by dark horsemen."

The dream or doctrine of the re-incarnation of souls,
which has given so much consolation to so many ques-
tioners of eternity, was for Gérard (need we doubt?) a
dream rather than a doctrine, but one of those dreams
which are nearer to a man than his breath. "This vague
and hopeless love," he writes in *Sylvie,* "inspired by an
actress, which night by night took hold of me at the hour
of the performance, leaving me only at the hour of sleep,
had its germ in the recollection of Adrienne, flower of
the night, unfolding under the pale rays of the moon,
rosy and blonde phantom, gliding over the green grass,
half bathed in white mist. . . . To love a nun under
the form of an actress! . . . and if it were the very

same! It is enough to drive one mad!" Yes, *il y a de quoi devenir fou,* as Gérard had found; but there was also, in this intimate sense of the unity, perpetuity, and harmoniously recurring rhythm of nature, not a little of the inner substance of wisdom. It was a dream, perhaps refracted from some broken, illuminating angle by which madness catches unseen light, that revealed to him the meaning of his own superstition, fatality, malady: "During my sleep, I had a marvellous vision. It seemed to me that the goddess appeared before me, saying to me: 'I am the same as Mary, the same as thy mother, the same also whom, under all forms, thou hast always loved. At each of thine ordeals I have dropt yet one more of the masks with which I veil my countenance, and soon thou shalt see me as I am!'" And in perhaps his finest sonnet, the mysterious *Artémis,* we have, under other symbols, and with the deliberate inconsequence of these sonnets, the comfort and despair of the same faith.

La Treizième revient . . . C'est encor la première;
Et c'est toujours la seule,—ou c'est le seul moment:
Car es-tu reine, ô toi! la première ou dernière?
Es-tu roi, toi le seul ou le dernier amant? . . .

Aimez qui vous aima du berceau dans la bière;
Celle que j'aimai seul m'aime encor tendrement;
C'est la mort—ou la morte . . . Ô délice! ô tourment!
La Rose qu'elle tient, c'est la Rose trémière.

Sainte napolitaine aux mains pleines de feux,
Rose au cœur violet, fleur de sainte Gudule:
As-tu trouvé ta croix dans le désert des cieux?

Roses blanches, tombez! vous insultez nos dieux:
Tombez, fantômes blancs, de votre ciel qui brûle:
—La Sainte de l'abîme est plus sainte à mes yeux!

Who has not often meditated, above all what artist, on the slightness, after all, of the link which holds our faculties together in that sober health of the brain which we call reason? Are there not moments when that link seems to be worn down to so fine a tenuity that the wing of a passing dream might suffice to snap it? The consciousness seems, as it were, to expand and contract at once, into something too wide for the universe, and too narrow for the thought of self to find room within it. Is it that the sense of identity is about to evaporate, annihilating all, or is it that a more profound identity, the identity of the whole sentient universe, has been at last realised? Leaving the concrete world on these brief voyages, the fear is that we may not have strength to return, or that we may lose the way back. Every artist lives a double life, in which he is for the most part conscious of the illusions of the imagination. He is conscious also of the illusions of the nerves, which he shares with every man of imaginative mind. Nights of insomnia, days of anxious waiting, the sudden shock of an event, any one of these common disturbances may be enough to jangle the tuneless bells of one's nerves. The artist can distinguish these causes of certain of his moods from those other causes which come to him because he is an artist, and are properly concerned with that invention which is his own function. Yet is there not some danger that he may come to confuse one with the other, that he may "lose the thread" which conducts him through the intricacies of the inner world?

The supreme artist, certainly, is the furthest of all men from this danger; for he is the supreme intelligence. Like Dante, he can pass through hell unsinged. With him, imagination is vision; when he looks into the darkness, he sees. The vague dreamer, the insecure artist and the uncertain mystic at once, sees only shadows, not recognising their outlines. He is mastered by the images which have come at his call; he has not the power which chains them for his slaves. "The kingdom of Heaven suffers violence," and the dreamer who has gone tremblingly into the darkness is in peril at the hands of those very real phantoms who are the reflection of his fear.

The madness of Gérard de Nerval, whatever physiological reasons may be rightly given for its outbreak, subsidence, and return, I take to have been essentially due to the weakness and not the excess of his visionary quality, to the insufficiency of his imaginative energy, and to his lack of spiritual discipline. He was an unsystematic mystic; his "Tower of Babel in two hundred volumes," that medley of books of religion, science, astrology, history, travel, which he thought would have rejoiced the heart of Pico della Mirandola, of Meursius, or of Nicholas of Cusa, was truly, as he says, "enough to drive a wise man mad." "Why not also," he adds, "enough to make a madman wise?" But precisely because it was this *amas bizarre,* this jumble of the perilous secrets in which wisdom is so often folly, and folly so often wisdom. He speaks vaguely of the Kabbala; the Kabbala would have been safety to him, as the Catholic Church would have been, or any other reasoned scheme of things. Wavering among intuitions, ignorances, half-truths, shadows of falsehood, now audacious, now hesitating, he was blown hither and thither by conflicting winds, a prey to the indefinite.

Le Rêve et la Vie, the last fragments of which were found in his pockets after his suicide, scrawled on scraps of paper, interrupted with Kabbalistic signs and "a demonstration of the Immaculate Conception by geometry," is a narrative of a madman's visions by the madman himself, yet showing, as Gautier says, "cold reason seated by the bedside of hot fever, hallucination analysing itself by a supreme philosophic effort." What is curious, yet after all natural, is that part of the narrative seems to be contemporaneous with what it describes, and part subsequent to it; so that it is not as when De Quincey says to us, such or such was the opium-dream that I had on such a night; but as if the opium-dreamer had begun to write down his dream while he was yet within its coils. "The descent into hell," he calls it twice; yet does he not also write: "At times I imagined that my force and my activity were doubled; it seemed to me that I knew everything, understood everything;

and imagination brought me infinite pleasures. Now that I have recovered what men call reason, must I not regret having lost them?" But he had not lost them; he was still in that state of double consciousness which he describes in one of his visions, when, seeing people dressed in white, "I was astonished," he says, "to see them all dressed in white; yet it seemed to me that this was an optical illusion." His cosmical visions are at times so magnificent that he seems to be creating myths; and it is with a worthy ingenuity that he plays the part he imagines to be assigned to him in his astral influences.

"First of all I imagined that the persons collected in the garden (of the madhouse) all had some influence on the stars, and that the one who always walked round and round in a circle regulated the course of the sun. An old man, who was brought there at certain hours of the day, and who made knots as he consulted his watch, seemed to me to be charged with the notation of the course of the hours. I attributed to myself an influence over the course of the moon, and I believed that this star had been struck by the thunderbolt of the Most High, which had traced on its face the imprint of the mask which I had observed.

"I attributed a mystical signification to the conversations of the warders and of my companions. It seemed to me that they were the representatives of all the races of the earth, and that we had undertaken between us to re-arrange the course of the stars, and to give a wider development to the system. An error, in my opinion, had crept into the general combination of numbers, and thence came all the ills of humanity. I believed also that the celestial spirits had taken human forms, and assisted at this general congress, seeming though they did to be concerned with but ordinary occupations. My own part seemed to me to be the re-establishment of universal harmony by Kabbalistic art, and I had to seek a solution by evoking the occult forces of various religions."

So far we have, no doubt, the confusions of madness,

in which what may indeed be the symbol is taken for the thing itself. But now observe what follows:

"I seemed to myself a hero living under the very eyes of the gods; everything in nature assumed new aspects, and secret voices came to me from the plants, the trees, animals, the meanest insects, to warn and to encourage me. The words of my companions had mysterious messages, the sense of which I alone understood; things without form and without life lent themselves to the designs of my mind; out of combinations of stones, the figures of angles, crevices, or openings, the shape of leaves, out of colours, odours, and sounds, I saw unknown harmonies come forth. 'How is it,' I said to myself, 'that I can possibly have lived so long outside nature, without identifying myself with her! All things live, all things are in motion, all things correspond; the magnetic rays emanating from myself or others traverse without obstacle the infinite chain of created things: a transparent network covers the world, whose loose threads communicate more and more closely with the planets and the stars. Now a captive upon the earth, I hold converse with the starry choir, which is feelingly a part of my joys and sorrows.'"

To have thus realized that central secret of the mystics, from Pythagoras onwards, the secret which the Smaragdine Tablet of Hermes betrays in its "As things are below, so are they above"; which Boehme has classed in his teaching of "signatures," and Swedenborg has systematised in his doctrine of "correspondences"; does it matter very much that he arrived at it by way of the obscure and fatal initiation of madness? Truth, and especially that soul of truth which is poetry, may be reached by many roads; and a road is not necessarily misleading because it is dangerous or forbidden. Here is one who has gazed at light till it has blinded him; and for us all that is important is that he has seen something, not that his eyesight has been too weak to endure the pressure of light overflowing from beyond the world.

III

And here we arrive at the fundamental principle which is at once the substance and the æsthetics of the sonnets "composed," as he explains, "in that state of meditation which the Germans would call 'supernaturalistic.'" In one, which I will quote, he is explicit, and seems to state a doctrine.

VERS DORÉS

Homme, libre penseur! te crois-tu seul pensant
Dans ce monde où la vie éclate en toute chose?
Des forces que tu tiens ta liberté dispose,
Mais de tous tes conseils l'univers est absent.

Respecte dans la bête un esprit agissant:
Chaque fleur est une âme à la Nature éclose;
Un mystère d'amour dans le métal repose;
"Tout est sensible!" Et tout sur ton être est puissant.

Crains, dans le mur aveugle un regard qui t'épie!
A la matière même un verbe est attaché . . .
Ne la fais pas servir à quelque usage impie!

Souvent dans l'être obscur habite un Dieu caché;
Et comme un œil naissant couvert par ses paupières,
Un pur esprit s'accroît sous l'écorce des pierres!

But in the other sonnets, in *Artémis*, which I have quoted, in *El Desdichado, Myrtho,* and the rest, he would seem to be deliberately obscure; or at least, his obscurity results, to some extent, from the state of mind which he describes in *Le Rêve et la Vie:* "I then saw, vaguely drifting into form, plastic images of antiquity, which outlined themselves, became definite, and seemed to represent symbols, of which I only seized the idea with difficulty." Nothing could more precisely represent the impression made by these sonnets, in which, for the first time in French, words are used as the ingredients of an evocation, as themselves not merely colour and sound, but symbol. Here are words which create an atmosphere by the actual suggestive quality of their syllables, as, according to the theory of Mallarmé, they should do; as, in the recent attempts of the Symbolists, writer after writer has endeavoured to lure them into doing. Persuaded, as Gérard was, of the sensitive unity of all nature, he was able to trace resemblances where others saw only divergences; and the setting together of unfamiliar and apparently alien things, which comes so strangely upon us in his verse, was perhaps an actual sight of what it is our misfortune not to see. His genius, to which madness had come as the liberating, the precipitating, spirit, disengaging its finer essence, consisted in a power of materialising vision, whatever is most volatile and unseizable in vision, and without losing the sense of mystery, or that quality which gives its charm to the intangible. Madness, then, in him, had lit up, as if by lightning-flashes, the hidden links of distant and divergent things; perhaps in somewhat the same manner as that in which a similarly new, startling, perhaps overtrue sight of things is gained by the artificial stimulation of hashish, opium, and those other drugs by which vision is produced deliberately, and the soul, sitting safe within the perilous circle of its own magic, looks out on the panorama which either rises out of the darkness before it, or drifts from itself into the darkness. The very imagery of these sonnets is the imagery which is known to all dreamers of bought dreams. *Rose au cœur violet, fleur de sainte Gudule; le Temple au péristyle immense; la grotte où nage la syrène:* the dreamer of bought dreams has seen them all. But no one before Gérard realised that such things as these might be the basis of almost a new æsthetics. Did he himself realise all that he had done, or was it left for Mallarmé to theorise upon what Gérard had but divined?

That he made the discovery, there is no doubt; and we owe to the fortunate accident of madness one of the foundations of what may be called the practical æsthetics of Symbolism. Look again at that sonnet *Artémis*, and you will see in it not only the method of Mallarmé, but much of the most intimate manner of Verlaine. The first four lines, with their fluid rhythm, their repetitions and echoes, their delicate evasions, might have been written by Verlaine; in the later part the firmness of the rhythms and the jewelled significance of the words are like Mallarmé at his finest, so that in a single sonnet we may fairly claim to see a foreshadowing of the styles of Mallarmé and Verlaine at once. With Verlaine the resemblance goes, perhaps, no further; with Mallarmé it goes to the very roots, the whole man being, certainly, his style.

Gérard de Nerval, then, had divined, before all the world, that poetry should be a miracle; not a hymn to beauty, nor the description of beauty, nor beauty's mirror; but beauty itself, the colour, fragrance, and form of the imagined flower, as it blossoms again out of the page. Vision, the over-powering vision, had come to him beyond, if not against, his will; and he knew that vision is the root out of which the flower must grow. Vision had taught him symbol, and he knew that it is by symbol alone that the flower can take visible form. He knew that the whole mystery of beauty can never be comprehended by the crowd, and that while clearness is a virtue of style, perfect explicitness is not a necessary virtue. So it was with disdain, as well as with confidence, that he allowed these sonnets to be overheard. It was enough for him to say:

> J'ai rêvé dans la grotte où nage la syrène;

and to speak, it might be, the siren's language, remembering her. "It will be my last madness," he wrote, "to believe myself a poet: let criticism cure me of it." Criticism, in his own day, even Gautier's criticism, could but be disconcerted by a novelty so unexampled. It is only now that the best critics in France are beginning to realise how great in themselves, and how great in their influence, are these sonnets, which, forgotten by the world for nearly fifty years, have all the while been secretly bringing new æsthetics into French poetry.

VILLIERS DE L'ISLE-ADAM

À chacun son infini

I

COUNT PHILIPPE AUGUSTE MATHIAS DE VILLIERS DE L'ISLE-ADAM was born at St. Brieuc, in Brittany, November 28, 1838; he died at Paris, under the care of the Frères Saint-Jean-de-Dieu, August 19, 1889. Even before his death, his life had become a legend, and the legend is even now not to be disentangled from the actual occurrences of an existence so heroically visionary. The Don Quixote of idealism, it was not only in philosophical terms that life, to him, was the dream, and the spiritual world the reality; he lived his faith, enduring what others called reality with contempt, whenever, for a moment, he became conscious of it. The basis of the character of Villiers was pride, and it was a pride which covered more than the universe. And this pride, first of all, was the pride of race.

Descendant of the original Rodolphe le Bel, Seigneur de Villiers (1067), through Jean de Villiers and Maria de l'Isle and their son Pierre the first Villiers de l'Isle-Adam, a Villiers de l'Isle-Adam, born in 1384, had been Marshal of France under Jeans-sans-Peur, Duke of Burgundy; he took Paris during the civil war, and after being imprisoned in the Bastille, reconquered Pontoise from the English, and helped to reconquer Paris. Another Villiers de l'Isle-Adam, born in 1464, Grand Master of the Order of St. John of Jerusalem, defended Rhodes against 200,000 Turks for a whole year, in one of the most famous sieges in history; it was he who obtained from Charles V the concession of the isle of Malta for his Order, henceforth the Order of the Knights of Malta.

For Villiers, to whom time, after all, was but a meta-physical abstraction, the age of the Crusaders had not passed. From a descendant of the Grand Master of the Knights of St. John of Jerusalem, the nineteenth century demanded precisely the virtues which the sixteenth century had demanded of that ancestor. And these virtues were all summed up in one word, which, in its double significance, single to him, covered the whole attitude of life: the word "nobility." No word returns oftener to the lips in speaking of what is most characteristic in his work, and to Villiers moral and spiritual nobility seemed but the inevitable consequence of that other kind of nobility by which he seemed to himself still a Knight of the Order of St. John of Jerusalem. It was his birth-right.

To the aristocratic conception of things, nobility of soul is indeed a birthright, and the pride with which this gift of nature is accepted is a pride of exactly the opposite kind to that democratic pride to which nobility of soul is a conquest, valuable in proportion to its difficulty. This duality, always essentially aristocratic and democratic, typically Eastern and Western also, finds its place in every theory of religion, philosophy, and the ideal life. The pride of *being,* the pride of *becoming:* these are the two ultimate contradictions set before every idealist. Villiers' choice, inevitable indeed, was signifi-cant. In its measure, it must always be the choice of the artist, to whom, in his contemplation of life, the means is often so much more important than the end. That nobility of soul which comes without effort, which comes only with an unrelaxed diligence over oneself, that I should be I: there can at least be no comparison of its beauty with the stained and dusty onslaught on a never quite conquered fort of the enemy, in a divided self. And, if it be permitted to choose among degrees of sanctity, that, surely, is the highest in which a natural genius for such things accepts its own attainment with the simplicity of a birthright.

And the Catholicism of Villiers was also a part of his inheritance. His ancestors had fought for the Church, and Catholicism was still a pompous flag, under which it was possible to fight on behalf of the spirit, against that materialism which is always, in one way or another, atheist. Thus he dedicates one of his stories to the Pope, chooses ecclesiastical splendours by preference among the many splendours of the world which go to make up his stage-pictures, and is learned in the subtleties of the Fathers. The Church is his favourite symbol of austere intellectual beauty; one way, certainly, by which the temptations of external matter may be vanquished, and a way, also, by which the desire of worship may be satisfied.

But there was also, in his attitude towards the mysteries of the spiritual world, that "forbidden" curiosity which had troubled the obedience of the Templars, and which came to him, too, as a kind of knightly quality. Whether or not he was actually a Kabbalist, questions of magic began, at an early age, to preoccupy him, and, from the first wild experiment of *Isis* to the deliberate summing up of *Axël*, the "occult" world finds its way into most of his pages.

Fundamentally, the belief of Villiers is the belief common to all Eastern mystics.[1] "Know, once for all, that there is for thee no other universe than that conception thereof which is reflected at the bottom of thy thoughts." "What is knowledge but a recognition?" Therefore, "forgetting for ever that which was the illusion of thyself," hasten to become "an intelligence freed from the bonds and the desires of the present moment." "Become the flower of thyself! Thou art but what thou thinkest: therefore think thyself eternal." "Man, if thou cease to limit in thyself a thing, that is, to desire it, if, so doing, thou withdraw thyself from it, it will follow thee, woman-like, as the water fills the place that is

[1] "I am far from sure," wrote Verlaine, "that the philosophy of Villiers will not one day become the formula of our century."

offered to it in the hollow of the hand. For thou possessest the real being of all things, in thy pure will, and thou art the God that thou art able to become."

To have accepted the doctrine which thus finds expression in *Axël,* is to have accepted this among others of its consequences: "Science states, but does not explain: she is the oldest offspring of the chimeras; all the chimeras, then, on the same terms as the world (the oldest of them!), are *something more* than nothing!" And in *Elën* there is a fragment of conversation between two young students, which has its significance also:

"*Goetze.* There's my philosopher in full flight to the regions of the sublime! Happily we have Science, which is a torch, dear mystic; we will analyse your sun, if the planet does not burst into pieces sooner than it has any right to!

Samuel. Science will not suffice. Sooner or later you will end by coming to your knees.

Goetze. Before what?

Samuel. Before the darkness!"

Such avowals of ignorance are possibly only from the height of a great intellectual pride. Villiers' revolt against Science, so far as Science is materialistic, and his passionate curiosity in that chimera's flight towards the invisible, are one and the same impulse of a mind to which only mind is interesting. *Toute cette vieille Extériorité, maligne, compliquée, inflexible,* that illusion which Science accepts for the one reality: it must be the whole effort of one's consciousness to escape from its entanglements, to dominate it, or to ignore it, and one's art must be the building of an ideal world beyond its access, from which one may indeed sally out, now and again, in a desperate enough attack upon the illusions in the midst of which men live.

And just that, we find, makes up the work of Villiers, work which divides itself roughly into two divisions: one, the ideal world, or the ideal in the world (*Axël, Elën,*

Morgane, Isis, some of the *contes,* and, intermediary,
La Révolte); the other, satire, the mockery of reality
(*L'Eve Future,* the *Contes Cruels, Tribulat Bonhomet*).
It is part of the originality of Villiers that the two divi-
sions constantly flow into one another; the idealist being
never more the idealist than in his buffooneries.

II

Axël is the Symbolist drama, in all its uncompromising
conflict with the "modesty" of Nature and the limitations
of the stage. It is the drama of the soul, and at the
same time it is the most pictorial of dramas; I should
define its manner as a kind of spiritual romanticism. The
earlier dramas, *Elën, Morgane,* are fixed at somewhat the
same point in space; *La Révolte,* which seems to anticipate *The Doll's House,* shows us an aristocratic Ibsen,
touching reality with a certain disdain, certainly with
far less skill, certainly with far more beauty. But *Axël,*
meditated over during a lifetime, shows us Villiers' ideal
of his own idealism.

The action takes place, it is true, in this century, but
it takes place in corners of the world into which the
modern spirit has not yet passed; this *Monastère de
Religieuses-trinitaires, le cloître de Sainte Apollodora,
situé sur les confins du littoral de l'ancienne Flandre
française,* and the *très vieux château fort, le burg des
margraves d'Auërsperg, isolé au milieu du Schwartzwald.*
The characters, Axël d'Auërsperg, Eve Sara Emmanuèle
de Maupers, Maître Janus, the Archidiacre, the Com-
mandeur Kaspar d'Auërsperg, are at once more and less
than human beings: they are the types of different ideals,
and they are clothed with just enough humanity to give
form to what would otherwise remain disembodied
spirit. The religious ideal, the occult ideal, the worldly
ideal, the passionate ideal, are all presented, one after the
other, in these dazzling and profound pages; Axël is the
disdainful choice from among them, the disdainful re-

jection of life itself, of the whole illusion of life, "since
infinity alone is not a deception." And Sara? Sara is a
superb part of that life which is rejected, which she herself comes, not without reluctance, to reject. In that
motionless figure, during the whole of the first act silent
but for a single "No," and leaping into a moment's
violent action as the act closes, she is the haughtiest
woman in literature. But she is a woman, and she desires
life, finding it in Axël. Pride, and the woman's devotion
to the man, aid her to take the last cold step with Axël,
in that transcendental giving up of life at the moment
when life becomes ideal.

And the play is written, throughout, with a curious
solemnity, a particular kind of eloquence, which makes
no attempt to imitate the level of the speech of every
day, but which is a sort of ideal language in which beauty
is aimed at as exclusively as if it were written in verse.
The modern drama, under the democratic influence of
Ibsen, the positive influence of Duman *fils,* has limited
itself to the expression of temperaments in the one case,
of theoretic intelligences in the other, in as nearly as
possible the words which the average man would use
for the statement of his emotions and ideas. The form,
that is, is degraded below the level of the characters
whom it attempts to express; for it is evident that the
average man can articulate only a small enough part of
what he obscurely feels or thinks; and the theory of
Realism is that his emotions and ideas are to be given
only in so far as the words at his own command can give
them. Villiers, choosing to concern himself only with
exceptional characters, and with them only in the absolute, invents for them a more elaborate and a more
magnificent speech than they would naturally employ,
the speech of their thoughts, of their dreams.

And it is a world thought or dreamt in some more
fortunate atmosphere than that in which we live, that
Villiers has created for the final achievement of his
abstract ideas. I do not doubt that he himself always

lived in it, through all the poverty of the precipitous
Rue des Martyrs. But it is in *Axël,* and in *Axël* only,
that he has made us also inhabitants of that world. Even
in *Elën* we are spectators, watching a tragical fairy play
(as if *Fantasio* became suddenly in deadly earnest), watching some one else's dreams. *Axël* envelops us in its own
atmosphere; it is as if we found ourselves on a mountain-
top, on the other side of the clouds, and without surprise
at finding ourselves there.

The ideal, to Villiers, being the real, spiritual beauty
being the essential beauty, and material beauty its reflection, or its revelation, it is with a sort of fury that he
attacks the materialising forces of the world: science,
progress, the worldly emphasis on "facts," on what is
"positive," "serious," "respectable." Satire, with him, is
the revenge of beauty upon ugliness, the persecution of
the ugly; it is not merely social satire, it is a satire on the
material universe by one who believes in a spiritual universe. Thus it is the only laughter of our time which is
fundamental, as fundamental as that of Swift or Rabelais.
And this lacerating laughter of the idealist is never surer
in its aim than when it turns the arms of science against
itself, as in the vast buffoonery of *L'Eve Future.* A
Parisian wit, sharpened to a fineness of irony such as only
wit which is also philosophy can attain, brings in another
method of attack; humour, which is almost English,
another; while again satire becomes tragic, fantastic,
macabre. In those enigmatic "tales of the grotesque and
arabesque," in which Villiers rivals Poe on his own
ground, there is, for the most part, a multiplicity of meaning which is, as it is meant to be, disconcerting. I should
not like to say how far Villiers does not, sometimes,
believe in his own magic.

It is characteristic of him, at all events, that he employs
what we call the supernatural alike in his works of pure
idealism and in his works of sheer satire. The moment
the world ceased to be the stable object, solidly encrusted
with houses in brick and stone, which it is to most of its

so temporary inhabitants, Villiers was at home. When he sought the absolute beauty, it was beyond the world that he found it; when he sought horror, it was a breath blowing from an invisible darkness which brought it to his nerves; when he desired to mock the pretensions of knowledge or of ignorance, it was always with the unseen that his tragic buffoonery made familiar.

There is, in everything which Villiers wrote, a strangeness, certainly both instinctive and deliberate, which seems to me to be the natural consequence of that intellectual pride which, as I have pointed out, was at the basis of his character. He hated every kind of mediocrity: therefore he chose to analyse exceptional souls, to construct exceptional stories, to invent splendid names, and to evoke singular landscapes. It was part of his curiosity in souls to prefer the complex to the simple, the perverse to the straightforward, the ambiguous to either. His heroes are incarnations of spiritual pride, and their tragedies are the shock of spirit against matter, the invasion of spirit by matter, the temptation of spirit by spiritual evil. They seek the absolute, and find death; they seek wisdom, find love, and fall into spiritual decay; they seek reality, and find crime; they seek phantoms, and find themselves. They are on the borders of a wisdom too great for their capacity; they are haunted by dark powers, instincts of ambiguous passions; they are too lucid to be quite sane in their extravagances; they have not quite systematically transposed their dreams into action. And his heroines, when they are not, like *L'Eve Future,* the vitalised mechanism of an Edison, have the solemnity of dead people, and a hieratic speech. *Songe, des cœurs condammés à ce supplice, de ne pas m'aimer!* says Sara, in *Axël. Je ne l'aime pas, ce jeune homme. Qu'ai-je donc fait à Dieu?* says Elën. And their voice is always like the voice of Elën: "I listened attentively to the sound of her voice; it was taciturn, subdued, like the murmur of the river Lethe, flowing through the region of shadows." They have the immortal weariness of beauty, they are enigmas to themselves, they desire, and know not why they refrain, they do good and evil with the lifting of an eyelid, and are innocent and guilty of all the sins of the earth.

And these strange inhabitants move in as strange a world. They are the princes and châtelaines of ancient castles lost in the depths of the Black Forest; they are the last descendants of a great race about to come to an end; students of magic, who have the sharp and swift swords of the soldier; enigmatic courtesans, at the table of strange feasts; they find incalculable treasures, *tonnantes et sonnantes cataractes d'or liquide,* only to disdain them. All the pomp of the world approaches them, that they may the better abnegate it, or that it may ruin them to a deeper degree of their material hell. And we see them always at the moment of a crisis, before the two ways of a decision, hesitating in the entanglements of a great temptation. And this casuist of souls will drag forth some horribly stunted or horribly overgrown soul from under its obscure covering, setting it to dance naked before our eyes. He has no mercy on those who have no mercy on themselves.

In the sense in which that word is ordinarily used, Villiers has no pathos. This is enough to explain why he can never, in the phrase he would have disliked so greatly, "touch the popular heart." His mind is too abstract to contain pity, and it is in his lack of pity that he seems to put himself outside humanity. *À chacun son infini,* he has said, and in the avidity of his search for the infinite he has no mercy for the blind weakness which goes stumbling over the earth, without so much as knowing that the sun and stars are overhead. He sees only the gross multitude, the multitude which has the contentment of the slave. He cannot pardon stupidity, for it is incomprehensible to him. He sees, rightly, that stupidity is more criminal than vice; if only because vice is curable, stupidity incurable. But he does not realise, as the great novelists have realised, that stupidity can be pathetic, and that there is not a peasant, nor even a self-satisfied bourgeois, in whom the soul has not its part, in whose existence it is not possible to be interested.

Contempt, noble as it may be, anger, righteous though it may be, cannot be indulged in without a certain lack of sympathy; and lack of sympathy comes from a lack of patient understanding. It is certain that the destiny of the greater part of the human race is either infinitely pathetic or infinitely ridiculous. Under which aspect, then, shall that destiny, and those obscure fractions of humanity, be considered? Villiers was too sincere an idealist, too absolute in his idealism, to hesitate. "As for living," he cries, in that splendid phrase of *Axël*, "our servants will do that for us!" And, in the *Contes Cruels*, there is this not less characteristic expression of what was always his mental attitude: "As at the play, in a central stall, one sits out, so as not to disturb one's neighbours —out of courtesy, in a word—some play written in a wearisome style and of which one does not like the subject, so I lived, out of politeness": *je vivais par politesse*. In this haughtiness towards life, in this disdain of ordinary human motives and ordinary human beings, there is at once the distinction and the weakness of Villiers. And he has himself pointed the moral against himself in these words of the story which forms the epiloque to the *Contes Cruels:* "When the forehead alone contains the existence of a man, that man is enlightened only from above his head; then his jealous shadow, prostrate under him, draws him by the feet, that it may drag him down into the invisible."

III

All his life Villiers was a poor man; though, all his life, he was awaiting that fortune which he refused to anticipate by any mean employment. During most of his life, he was practically an unknown man. Greatly loved, ardently admired, by that inner circle of the men who

have made modern French literature, from Verlaine to
Maeterlinck, he was looked upon by most people as an
amusing kind of madman, a little dangerous, whose ideas,
as they floated freely over the café-table, it was at times
highly profitable to steal. For Villiers talked his works
before writing them, and sometimes he talked them
instead of writing them, in his too royally spendthrift
way. To those who knew him he seemed genius itself,
and would have seemed so if he had never written a line;
for he had the dangerous gift of a personality which
seems to have already achieved all that it so energetically
contemplates. But personality tells only within hands'
reach; and Villiers failed even to startle, failed even to
exasperate, the general reader. That his *Premières
Poésies*, published at the age of nineteen, should have
brought him fame was hardly to be expected, remarkable,
especially in its ideas, as that book is. Nor was it to be
expected of the enigmatic fragment of a romance, *Isis*
(1862), anticipating, as it does, by so long a period, the
esoteric and spiritualistic romances which were to have
their vogue. But *Elën* (1864) and *Morgane* (1865), those
two poetic dramas in prose, so full of distinction, of
spiritual rarity; but two years later, *Claire Lenoir* (afterwards incorporated in one of his really great books,
Tribulat Bonhomet), with its macabre horror; but *La
Révolte* (1870), for Villiers so "actual," and which had its
moment's success when it was revived in 1896 at the
Odéon; but *Le Nouveau Monde* (1880), a drama which,
by some extraordinary caprice, won a prize; but *Les
Contes Cruels* (1880), that collection of masterpieces, in
which the essentially French *conte* is outdone on its own
ground! It was not till 1886 that Villiers ceased to be an
unknown writer, with the publication of that phosphores-
cent buffoonery of science, that vast parody of humanity,
L'Eve Future. *Tribulat Bonhomet* (which he himself
defined as *bouffonnerie énorme et sombre, couleur du
siècle*) was to come, in its final form, and the superb poem
in prose *Akëdysséril;* and then, more and more indifferent

collections of stories, in which Villiers, already dying, is but the shadow of himself: *L'Amour Suprême* (1886), *Histoires Insolites* (1888), *Nouveaux Contes Cruels* (1888). He was correcting the proofs of *Axël* when he died; the volume was published in 1890, followed by *Propos d'audelà,* and a series of articles, *Chez les Passants.* Once dead, the fame which had avoided him all his life began to follow him; he had *une belle presse* at his funeral.

Meanwhile, he had been preparing the spiritual atmosphere of the new generation. Living among believers in the material world, he had been declaring, not in vain, his belief in the world of the spirit; living among Realists and Parnassians, he had been creating a new form of art, the art of the Symbolist drama, and of Symbolism in fiction. He had been lonely all his life, for he had been living, in his own lifetime, the life of the next generation. There was but one man among his contemporaries to whom he could give, and from whom he could receive, perfect sympathy. That man was Wagner. Gradually the younger men came about him; at the end he was not lacking in disciples.

And after all, the last word of Villiers is faith; faith against the evidence of the senses, against the negations of materialistic science, against the monstrous paradox of progress, against his own pessimism in the face of these formidable enemies. He affirms; he "believes in soul, is very sure of God"; requires no witness to the spiritual world of which he is always the inhabitant; and is content to lose his way in the material world, brushing off its mud from time to time with a disdainful gesture, as he goes on his way (to apply a significant word of Pater) "like one on a secret errand."

ARTHUR RIMBAUD

THAT story of the Arabian Nights, which is at the same time a true story, the life of Rimbaud, has been told, for the first time, in the extravagant but valuable book of an anarchist of letters, who writes under the name of Paterne Berrichon, and who has since married Rimbaud's sister. *La Vie de Jean-Arthur Rimbaud* is full of curiosity for those who have been mystified by I know not what legends, invented to give wonder to a career, itself more wonderful than any of the inventions. The man who died at Marseilles, at the Hospital of the Conception, on March 10, 1891, at the age of thirty-seven, *négociant*, as the register of his death describes him, was a writer of genius, an innovator in verse and prose, who had written all his poetry by the age of nineteen, and all his prose by a year or two later. He had given up literature to travel hither and thither, first in Europe, then in Africa; he had been an engineer, a leader of caravans, a merchant of precious merchandise. And this man, who had never written down a line after those astonishing early experiments, was heard, in his last delirium, talking of precisely such visions as those which had haunted his youth, and using, says his sister, "expressions of a singular and penetrating charm" to render these sensations of visionary countries. Here certainly is one of the most curious problems of literature: is it a problem of which we can discover the secret?

Jean-Nicolas-Arthur Rimbaud was born at Charleville, in the Ardennes, October 28, 1854. His father, of whom he saw little, was a captain in the army; his mother, of peasant origin, was severe, rigid, and unsympathetic. At school he was an unwilling but brilliant scholar, and by his fifteenth year was well acquainted with Latin literature and intimately with French literature. It was in that year that he began to write poems, from the first curiously original: eleven poems dating from that year are to be found in his collected works. When he was sixteen he decided that he had had enough of school, and enough of home. Only Paris existed: he must go to Paris. The first time he went without a ticket; he spent, indeed, fifteen days in Paris, but he spent them in Mazas, from which he was released and restored to his home by his schoolmaster. The second time, a few days later, he sold his watch, which paid for his railway ticket. This time he threw himself on the hospitality of André Gill, a painter and verse-writer, of some little notoriety then, whose address he had happened to come across. The uninvited guest was not welcomed, and after some penniless days in Paris he tramped back to Charleville. The third time (he had waited five months, writing poems, and discontented to be only writing poems) he made his way to Paris on foot, in a heat of revolutionary sympathy, to offer himself to the insurgents of the Commune. Again he had to return on foot. Finally, having learnt with difficulty that a man is not taken at his own valuation until he has proved his right to be so accepted, he sent up the manuscript of his poems to Verlaine. The manuscript contained *Le Bateau Ivre, Les Premières Communions, Ma Bohème, Roman, Les Effarés,* and, indeed, all but a few of the poems he ever wrote. Verlaine was overwhelmed with delight, and invited him to Paris. A local admirer lent him the money to get there, and from October 1871 to July 1872 he was Verlaine's guest.

The boy of seventeen, already a perfectly original poet, and beginning to be an equally original prose-writer, astonished the whole Parnasse, Banville, Hugo himself. On Verlaine his influence was more profound. The meeting brought about one of those lamentable and admirable disasters which make and unmake careers. Verlaine has told us in his *Confessions* that, "in the beginning, there was no question of any sort of affection or sympathy between two natures so different as that of the poet of the *Assis* and mine, but simply of an extreme admiration and astonishment before this boy of sixteen, who had already written things, as Fénélon has excellently said, 'perhaps outside literature.'" This admiration and astonishment passed gradually into a more personal feeling, and it was under the influence of Rimbaud that the long vagabondage of Verlaine's life began. The two poets wandered together through Belgium, England, and again Belgium, from July 1872 to August 1873, when there occurred that tragic parting at Brussels which left Verlaine a prisoner for eighteen months, and sent Rimbaud back to his family. He had already written all the poetry and prose that he was ever to write, and in 1873 he printed at Brussels *Une Saison en Enfer*. It was the only book he himself ever gave to the press, and no sooner was it printed than he destroyed the whole edition, with the exception of a few copies, of which only Verlaine's copy, I believe, still exists. Soon began new wanderings, with their invariable return to the starting-point of Charleville: a few days in Paris, a year in England, four months in Stuttgart (where he was visited by Verlaine), Italy, France again, Vienna, Java, Holland, Sweden, Egypt, Cyprus, Abyssinia, and then nothing but Africa, until the final return to France. He had been a teacher of French in England, a seller of key-rings in the streets of Paris, had unloaded vessels in the ports, and helped to gather in the harvest in the country; he had been a volunteer in the Dutch army, a military engineer, a trader; and now physical sciences had begun to attract his insatiable curiosity, and dreams of the fabulous East began to resolve themselves into dreams of a romantic commerce with the real East. He became a merchant of coffee, perfumes, ivory, and gold, in the interior of Africa; then an explorer, a predecessor, and in his own regions, of Marchand. After twelve years' wandering and exposure in Africa he was attacked by a malady of the knee, which rapidly became worse. He was transported first to Aden, then to Marseilles, where, in May 1891, his leg was amputated. Further complications set in. He insisted, first, on being removed to his home, then on being taken back to Marseilles. His sufferings were an intolerable torment, and more cruel to him was the torment of his desire to live. He died inch by inch, fighting every inch; and his sister's quiet narrative of those last months is agonising. He died at Marseilles in November, "prophesying," says his sister, and repeating, "Allah Kerim! Allah Kerim!"

The secret of Rimbaud, I think, and the reason why he was able to do the unique thing in literature which he did, and then to disappear quietly and become a legend in the East, is that his mind was not the mind of the artist but of the man of action. He was a dreamer, but all his dreams were discoveries. To him it was an identical act of his temperament to write the sonnet of the *Vowels* and to trade in ivory and frankincense with the Arabs. He lived with all his faculties at every instant of his life, abandoning himself to himself with a confidence which was at once his strength and (looking at things less absolutely) his weakness. To the student of success, and what is relative in achievement, he illustrates the danger of one's over-possession by one's own genius, just as aptly as the saint in the cloister does, or the mystic too full of God to speak intelligibly to the world, or the spilt wisdom of the drunkard. The artist who is above all things an artist cultivates a little choice corner of himself with elaborate care; he brings miraculous flowers to growth there, but the rest of the garden is but mown grass or tangled bushes. That is why many excellent writers, very many painters, and most musicians are so tedious on any subject but their own. Is it not tempting, does it not seem a devotion rather than a superstition, to worship the golden chalice in which the wine has been made God, as if the chalice were the reality, and the Real Presence the symbol? The artist, who is only an artist, circumscribes his intelligence into almost such a fiction, as he reverences the work of his own hands. But there are certain natures (great or small, Shakespeare or Rimbaud, it makes no difference) to whom the work is nothing; the act of working, everything. Rimbaud was a small, narrow, hard, precipitate nature, which had the will to live, and nothing but the will to live; and his verses, and his follies, and his wanderings, and his

In all these ways, Rimbaud had his influence upon Verlaine, and his influence upon Verlaine was above all the influence of the man of action upon the man of sensation; the influence of what is simple, narrow, emphatic, upon what is subtle, complex, growing. Verlaine's rich, sensitive nature was just then trying to realise itself. Just because it had such delicate possibilities, because there were so many directions in which it could grow, it was not at first quite sure of its way. Rimbaud came into the life and art of Verlaine, troubling both, with that trouble which reveals a man to himself. Having helped to make Verlaine a great poet, he could go. Note that he himself could never have developed: writing had been one of his discoveries; he could but make other discoveries, personal ones. Even in literature he had his future; but his future was Verlaine.

PAUL VERLAINE

I

"BIEN affectueusement . . . yours, P. Verlaine." So, in its gay and friendly mingling of French and English, ended the last letter I had from Verlaine. A few days afterwards came the telegram from Paris telling me of his death, in the Rue Descartes, on that 8th January 1896.

"Condemned to death," as he was, in Victor Hugo's phrase of men in general, "with a sort of indefinite reprieve," and gravely ill as I had for some time known him to be, it was still with a shock, not only of sorrow, but of surprise, that I heard the news of his death. He had suffered and survived so much, and I found it so hard to associate the idea of death with one who had always been so passionately in love with life, more passionately in love with life than any man I ever knew. Rest was one of the delicate privileges of life which he never loved: he did but endure it with grumbling gaiety when a hospital-bed claimed him. And whenever he spoke to me of the long rest which has now sealed his eyelids, it was with a shuddering revolt from the thought of ever going away into the cold, out of the sunshine which had been so warm to him. With all his pains, misfortunes, and the calamities which followed him step by step all his life, I think few men ever got so much out of their lives, or lived so fully, so intensely, with such a genius for living. That, indeed, is why he was a great poet. Verlaine was a man who gave its full value to every moment, who got out of every moment all that that moment had to give him. It was not always, not often, perhaps, pleasure. But it was energy, the vital force of a nature which was always receiving and giving out, never at rest, never passive, or indifferent, or hesitating. It is impossible for me to convey to those who did not know him any notion of how sincere he was. The word "sincerity" seems hardly to have emphasis enough to say, in regard to this one man, what it says, adequately enough, of others. He sinned, and it was with all his humanity; he repented, and it was with all his soul. And to every occurrence of the day, to every mood of the mind, to every impulse of the creative instinct, he brought the same unparalleled sharpness of sensation. When, in 1894, he was my guest in London, I was amazed by the exactitude of his memory of the mere turnings of the streets, the shapes and colours of the buildings, which he had not seen for twenty years. He saw, he felt, he remembered, everything, with an unconscious mental selection of the fine shades, the essential part of things, or precisely those aspects which most other people would pass by.

Few poets of our time have been more often drawn, few have been easier to draw, few have better repaid drawing, than Paul Verlaine. A face without a beautiful line, a face all character, full of somnolence and sudden fire, in which every irregularity was a kind of aid to the hand, could not but tempt the artist desiring at once to render a significant likeness and to have his own part in the creation of a picture. Verlaine, like all men of

genius, had something of the air of the somnambulist:
that profound slumber of the face, as it was in him,
with its startling awakenings. It was a face devoured by
dreams, feverish and somnolent; it had earthly passion,
intellectual pride, spiritual humility; the air of one who
remembers, not without an effort, who is listening, half
distractedly to something which other people do not hear;
coming back so suddenly, and from so far, with the relief
of one who steps out of that obscure shadow into the
noisier forgetfulness of life. The eyes, often half closed,
were like the eyes of a cat between sleeping and waking;
eyes in which contemplation was "itself an act." A
remarkable lithograph by Mr. Rothenstein (the face lit
by oblique eyes, the folded hand thrust into the cheek)
gives with singular truth the sensation of that restless
watch on things which this prisoner of so many chains
kept without slackening. To Verlaine every corner of
the world was alive with tempting and consoling and
terrifying beauty. I have never known any one to whom
the sight of the eyes was so intense and imaginative a
thing. To him, physical sight and spiritual vision, by
some strange alchemical operation of the brain, were one.
And in the disquietude of his face, which seemed to take
such close heed of things, precisely because it was sufficiently apart from them to be always a spectator, there
was a realisable process of vision continually going on, in
which all the loose ends of the visible world were being
caught up into a new mental fabric.

And along with this fierce subjectivity, into which the
egoism of the artist entered so unconsciously, and in
which it counted for so much, there was more than the
usual amount of childishness, always in some measure
present in men of genius. There was a real, almost
blithe, childishness in the way in which he would put
on his "Satanic" expression, of which it was part of the
joke that every one should not be quite in the secret. It
was a whim of this kind which made him put at the beginning of *Romances sans Paroles* that very criminal

image of a head which had so little resemblance with even the shape, indeed curious enough, of his actual head. "Born under the sign of Saturn," as he no doubt was, with that "old prisoner's head" of which he tells us, it was by his amazing faculty for a simple kind of happiness that he always impressed me. I have never seen so cheerful an invalid as he used to be at that hospital, the Hôpital Saint-Louis, where at one time I used to go and see him every week. His whole face seemed to chuckle as he would tell me, in his emphatic, confiding way, everything that entered into his head; the droll stories cut short by a groan, a lamentation, a sudden fury of reminiscence, at which his face would cloud or convulse, the wild eyebrows slanting up and down; and then, suddenly, the good laugh would be back, clearing the air. No one was ever so responsive to his own moods as Verlaine, and with him every mood had the vehemence of a passion. Is not his whole art a delicate waiting upon moods, with that perfect confidence in them as they are, which it is a large part of ordinary education to discourage in us, and a large part of experience to repress? But to Verlaine, happily, experience taught nothing; or rather, it taught him only to cling the more closely to those moods in whose succession lies the more intimate part of our spiritual life.

It is no doubt well for society that man should learn by experience; for the artist the benefit is doubtful. The artist, it cannot be too clearly understood, has no more part in society than a monk in domestic life: he cannot be judged by its rules, he can be neither praised nor blamed for his acceptance or rejection of its conventions. Social rules are made by normal people for normal people, and the man of genius is fundamentally abnormal. It is the poet against society, society against the poet, a direct antagonism; the shock of which, however, it is often possible to avoid by a compromise. So much licence is allowed on the one side, so much liberty foregone on the other. The consequences are not always of the best, art being generally the loser. But there are certain natures to which compromise is impossible; and the nature of Verlaine was one of these natures.

"The soul of an immortal child," says one who has understood him better than others, Charles Morice, "that is the soul of Verlaine, with all the privileges and all the perils of so being: with the sudden despair so easily distracted, the vivid gaieties without a cause, the excessive suspicions and the excessive confidences, the whims so easily outwearied, the deaf and blind infatuations, with, especially, the unceasing renewal of impressions in the incorruptible integrity of personal vision and sensation. Years, influences, teachings, may pass over a temperament such as this, may irritate it, may fatigue it; transform it, never—never so much as to alter that particular unity which consists in a dualism, in the division of forces between the longing after what is evil and the adoration of what is good; or rather, in the antagonism of spirit and flesh. Other men 'arrange' their lives, take sides, follow one direction; Verlaine hesitates before a choice, which seems to him monstrous, for, with the integral *naïveté* of irrefutable human truth, he cannot resign himself, however strong may be the doctrine, however enticing may be the passion, to the necessity of sacrificing one to the other, and from one to the other he oscillates without a moment's repose."

It is in such a sense as this that Verlaine may be said to have learnt nothing from experience, in the sense that he learnt everything direct from life, and without comparing day with day. That the exquisite artist of the *Fêtes Galantes* should become the great poet of *Sagesse*, it was needful that things should have happened as disastrously as they did: the marriage with the girl-wife, that brief idyl, the passion for drink, those other forbidden passions, vagabondage, an attempted crime, the eighteen months of prison, conversion; followed, as it had to be, by relapse, bodily sickness, poverty, beggary almost, a lower and lower descent into mean distresses. It was needful that all this should happen, in order that the spiritual vision should eclipse the material vision; but it was needful that all this should happen in vain, so far as the conduct of life was concerned. Reflection, in Verlaine, is pure waste; it is the speech of the soul and the speech of the eyes, that we must listen to in his verse, never the speech of the reason. And I call him fortunate because, going through life with a great unconsciousness of what most men spend their lives in considering, he was able to abandon himself entirely to himself, to his unimpeded vision, to his unchecked emotion, to the passionate sincerity which in him was genius.

II

French poetry, before Verlaine, was an admirable vehicle for a really fine, a really poetical, kind of rhetoric. With Victor Hugo, for the first time since Ronsard (the two or three masterpieces of Ronsard and his companions) it had learnt to sing; with Baudelaire it had invented a new vocabulary for the expression of subtle, often perverse, essentially modern emotion and sensation. But with Victor Hugo, with Baudelaire, we are still under the dominion of rhetoric. "Take eloquence, and wring its neck!" said Verlaine in his *Art Poétique;* and he showed, by writing it, that French verse could be written without rhetoric. It was partly from his study of English models that he learnt the secret of liberty in verse, but it was much more a secret found by the way, in the mere endeavour to be absolutely sincere, to express exactly what he saw, to give voice to his own temperament, in which intensity of feeling seemed to find its own expression, as if by accident. *L'art, mes enfants, c'est d'être absolument soi-même,* he tells us in one of his later poems; and, with such a personality as Verlaine's to express, what more has art to do, if it would truly, and in any interesting manner, hold the mirror up to nature? For, consider the natural qualities which this man had for the task of creating a new poetry. "Sincerity, and the impression of the moment followed to the letter": that is how he defined his theory of style, in an article written about himself.

> Car nous voulons la nuance encor,
> Pas la couleur, rien que la nuance!

as he cries, in his famous *Art Poétique*. Take, then, his susceptibility of the senses, an emotional susceptibility not less delicate; a life sufficiently troubled to draw out every emotion of which he was capable, and, with it, that absorption in the moment, that inability to look before or after; the need to love and the need to confess, each a passion; an art of painting the fine shades of landscape, of evoking atmosphere, which can be compared only with the art of Whistler; a simplicity of language which is the direct outcome of a simplicity of temperament, with just enough consciousness of itself for a final elegance; and, at the very depth of his being, an almost fierce humility, by which the passion of love, after searching furiously through all his creatures, finds God by the way, and kneels in the dust before him. Verlaine was never a theorist: he left theories to Mallarmé. He had only his divination; and he divined that poetry, always desiring that miracles should happen, had never waited patiently enough upon the miracle. It was by that proud and humble mysticism of his temperament that he came to realise how much could be done by, in a sense, trying to do nothing.

And then: *De la musique avant toute chose; De la musique encore et toujours!* There are poems of Verlaine which go as far as verse can go to become pure music, the voice of a bird with a human soul. It is part of his simplicity, his divine childishness, that he abandons himself, at times, to the song which words begin to sing in the air, with the same wise confidence with which he abandons himself to the other miracles about him. He knows that words are living things, which we have not

created, and which go their way without demanding of us
the right to live. He knows that words are suspicious, not
without their malice, and that they resist mere force
with the impalpable resistance of fire or water. They are
to be caught only with guile or with trust. Verlaine has
both, and words become Ariel to him. They bring him
not only that submission of the slave which they bring
to others, but all the soul, and in a happy bondage. They
transform themselves for him into music, colour, and
shadow; a disembodied music, diaphanous colours,
luminous shadow. They serve him with so absolute a
self-negation that he can write *romances sans paroles,*
songs almost without words, in which scarcely a sense of
the interference of human speech remains. The ideal of
lyric poetry, certainly, is to be this passive, flawless
medium for the deeper consciousness of things, the
mysterious voice of that mystery which lies about us, out
of which we have come, and into which we shall return.
It is not without reason that we cannot analyse a perfect
lyric.

With Verlaine the sense of hearing and the sense of
sight are almost interchangeable: he paints with sound,
and his line and atmosphere become music. It was with
the most precise accuracy that Whistler applied the
terms of music to his painting, for painting, when it aims
at being the vision of reality, *pas la couleur, rien que la
nuance,* passes almost into the condition of music. Verlaine's landscape painting is always an evocation, in
which outline is lost in atmosphere.

> C'est des beaux yeux derrière des voiles,
>   C'est le grand jour tremblant de midi,
>   C'est, par un ciel d'automne attiédi,
> Le bleu fouillis des claires étoiles!

He was a man, certainly, "for whom the visible world
existed," but for whom it existed always as a vision. He
absorbed it through all his senses, as the true mystic
absorbs the divine beauty. And so he created in verse a

new voice for nature, full of the humble ecstasy with which he saw, listened, accepted.

> Cette âme qui se lamente
> En cette plaine dormante
>   C'est la nôtre, n'est-ce pas?
> La mienne, dis, et la tienne,
> Dont s'exhale l'humble antienne
>   Par ce tiède soir, tout bas?

And with the same attentive simplicity with which he found words for the sensations of hearing and the sensations of sight, he found words for the sensations of the soul, for the fine shades of feeling. From the moment when his inner life may be said to have begun, he was occupied with the task of an unceasing confession, in which one seems to overhear him talking to himself, in that vague, preoccupied way which he often had. Here again are words which startle one by their delicate resemblance to thoughts, by their winged flight from so far, by their alighting so close. The verse murmurs, with such an ingenuous confidence, such intimate secrets. That "setting free" of verse, which is one of the achievements of Verlaine, was itself mainly an attempt to be more and more sincere, a way of turning poetic artifice to new account, by getting back to nature itself, hidden away under the eloquent rhetoric of Hugo, Baudelaire, and the Parnassians. In the devotion of rhetoric to either beauty or truth, there is a certain consciousness of an audience, of an external judgment: rhetoric would convince, be admired. It is the very essence of poetry to be unconscious of anything between its own moment of flight and the supreme beauty which it will never attain. Verlaine taught French poetry that wise and subtle unconsciousness. It was in so doing that he "fused his personality," in the words of Verhaeren, "so profoundly with beauty, that he left upon it the imprint of a new and henceforth eternal attitude."

III

J'ai la fureur d'aimer, says Verlaine, in a passage of very personal significance.

> J'ai la fureur d'aimer. Mon cœur si faible est fou.
> N'importe quand, n'importe quel et n'importe où,
> Qu'un éclair de beauté, de vertu, de vaillance,
> Luise, il s'y précipite, il y vole, il y lance,
> Et, le temps d'une étreinte, il embrasse cent fois
> L'être ou l'objet qu'il a poursuivi de son choix;
> Puis, quand l'illusion a replié son aile,
> Il revient triste et seul bien souvent, mais fidèle,
> Et laissant aux ingrats quelque chose de lui,
> Sang ou chair . . . .
> J'ai la fureur d'aimer. Qu'y faire? Ah, laissez faire!

And certainly this admirable, and supremely dangerous, quality was at the root of Verlaine's nature. Instinctive, unreasoning as he was, entirely at the mercy of the emotion or impression which, for the moment, had seized upon him, it was inevitable that he should be completely at the mercy of the most imperious of instincts, of passions, and of intoxications. And he had the simple and ardent nature, in this again consistently childlike, to which love, some kind of affection, given or returned, is not the luxury, the exception, which it is to many natures, but a daily necessity. To such a temperament there may or may not be the one great passion; there will certainly be many passions. And in Verlaine I find that single, childlike necessity of loving and being loved, all through his life and on every page of his works; I find it, unchanged in essence, but constantly changing form, in his chaste and unchaste devotions to women, in his passionate friendships with men, in his supreme mystical adoration of God.

To turn from *La Bonne Chanson,* written for a wedding present to a young wife, to *Chansons pour Elle,* written more than twenty years later, in dubious honour

of a middle-aged mistress, is to travel a long road, the
hard, long road which Verlaine had travelled during
those years. His life was ruinous, a disaster, more sordid
perhaps than the life of any other poet; and he could
write of it, from a hospital-bed, with this quite sufficient
sense of its deprivations. "But all the same, it is hard,"
he laments, in *Mes Hôpitaux*, "after a life of work, set
off, I admit, with accidents in which I have had a large
share, catastrophes perhaps vaguely premeditated—it is
hard, I say, at forty-seven years of age, in full possession
of all the reputation (of the *success*, to use the frightful
current phrase) to which my highest ambitions could
aspire—hard, hard, hard indeed, worse than hard, to find
myself—good God!—to find myself *on the streets*, and
to have nowhere to lay my head and support an ageing
body save the pillows and the *menus* of a public charity,
even now uncertain, and which might at any moment
be withdrawn—God forbid!—without, apparently, the
fault of any one, oh! not even, and above all, not mine."
Yet, after all, these sordid miseries, this poor man's vagabondage, all the misfortunes of one certainly "irreclaim-
able," on which so much stress has been laid, alike by
friends and by foes, are externalities; they are not the
man; the man, the eternal lover, passionate and humble,
remains unchanged, while only his shadow wanders, from
morning to night of the long day.

The poems to Rimbaud, to Lucien Létinois, to others,
the whole volume of *Dédicaces*, cover perhaps as wide a
range of sentiment as *La Bonne Chanson* and *Chansons
pour Elle*. The poetry of friendship has never been sung
with such plaintive sincerity, such simple human feeling,
as in some of these poems, which can only be compared,
in modern poetry, with a poem for which Verlaine had a
great admiration, Tennyson's *In Memoriam*. Only, with
Verlaine, the thing itself, the affection or the regret, is
everything; there is no room for meditation over destiny,
or search for a problematical consolation. Other poems
speak a more difficult language, in which, doubtless,

l'ennui de vivre avec les gens et dans les choses counts for much, and *la fureur d'aimer* for more.

In spite of the general impression to the contrary, an impression which by no means displeased him himself, I must contend that the sensuality of Verlaine, brutal as it could sometimes be, was after all simple rather than complicated, instinctive rather than perverse. In the poetry of Baudelaire, with which the poetry of Verlaine is so often compared, there is a deliberate science of sensual perversity which has something almost monachal in its accentuation of vice with horror, in its passionate devotion to passions. Baudalaire brings every complication of taste, the exasperation of perfumes, the irritant of cruelty, the very odours and colours of corruption, to the creation and adornment of a sort of religion, in which an eternal mass is served before a veiled altar. There is no confession, no absolution, not a prayer is permitted which is not set down in the ritual. With Verlaine, however often love may pass into sensuality, to whatever length sensuality may be hurried, sensuality is never more than the malady of love. It is love desiring the absolute, seeking in vain, seeking always, and, finally, out of the depths, finding God.

Verlaine's conversion took place while he was in prison, during those solitary eighteen months in company with his thoughts, that enforced physical inactivity, which could but concentrate his whole energy on the only kind of sensation then within his capacity, the sensations of the soul and of the conscience. With that promptitude of abandonment which was his genius, he grasped feverishly at the succour of God and the Church, he abased himself before the immaculate purity of the Virgin. He had not, like others who have risen from the same depths to the same height of humiliation, to despoil his nature of its pride, to conquer his intellect, before he could become *l'enfant vêtu de laine et d'innocence*. All that was simple, humble, childlike in him accepted that humiliation with the loving child's joy in penitence; all that was ardent, impulsive, indomitable in him burst at once into a flame of adoration.

He realised the great secret of the Christian mystics: that it is possible to love God with an extravagance of the whole being, to which the love of the creature cannot attain. All love is an attempt to break through the loneliness of individuality, to fuse oneself with something not oneself, to give and to receive, in all the warmth of natural desire, that inmost element which remains, so cold and so invincible, in the midst of the soul. It is a desire of the infinite in humanity, and, as humanity has its limits, it can but return sadly upon itself when that limit is reached. Thus human love is not only an ecstasy but a despair, and the more profound a despair the more ardently it is returned.

But the love of God, considered only from its human aspect, contains at least the illusion of infinity. To love God is to love the absolute, so far as the mind of man can conceive the absolute, and thus, in a sense, to love God is to possess the absolute, for love has already possessed that which it apprehends. What the earthly lover realises to himself as the image of his beloved, is, after all, his own vision of love, not her. God must remain *deus absconditus,* even to love; but the lover, incapable of possessing infinity, will have possessed all of infinity of which he is capable. And his ecstasy will be flawless. The human mind, meditating on infinity, can but discover perfection beyond perfection; for it is impossible to conceive of limitation in any aspect of that which has once been conceived as infinite. In place of that deception which comes from the shock of a boundary-line beyond which humanity cannot conceive of humanity, there is only a divine rage against the limits of human perception, which by their own failure seem at last to limit for us the infinite itself. For once, love finds itself bounded only by its own capacity; so far does the

love of God exceed the love of the creature, and so far
would it exceed that love if God did not exist.

But if he does exist! if, outside humanity, a conscient,
eternal perfection, who has made the world in his image,
loves the humanity he has made, and demands love in
return! If the spirit of his love is as a breath over the
world, suggesting, strengthening, the love which it desires, seeking man that man may seek God, itself the
impulse which it humbles itself to accept at man's hands;
if, indeed,

> Mon Dieu m'a dit: mon fils, il faut m'aimer;

how much more is this love of God, in its inconceivable
acceptance and exchange, the most divine, the only un-
ending, intoxication in the world! Well, it is this realised
sense of communion, point by point realised, and put
into words, more simple, more human, more instinctive
than any poet since the mediæval mystics has found for
the delights of this intercourse, that we find in *Sagesse,*
and in the other religious poems of Verlaine.

But, with Verlaine, the love of God is not merely a
rapture, it is a thanksgiving for forgiveness. Lying in wait
behind all the fair appearances of the world, he remembers the old enemy, the flesh; and the sense of sin (that
strange paradox of the reason) is childishly strong in him.
He laments his offence, he sees not only the love but the
justice of God, and it seems to him, as in a picture, that
the little hands of the Virgin are clasped in petition for
him. Verlaine's religion is the religion of the Middle
Ages. *Je suis catholique,* he said to me, *mais . . .
catholique du moyen-âge!* He might have written the
ballad which Villon made for his mother, and with the
same visual sense of heaven and hell. Like a child, he
tells his sins over, promises that he has put them behind
him, and finds such *naïve,* human words to express his
gratitude. The Virgin is really, to him, mother and
friend; he delights in the simple, peasant humanity, still

visible in her who is also the Mystical Rose, the Tower of Ivory, the Gate of Heaven, and who now extends her hands, in the gesture of pardon, from a throne only just lower than the throne of God.

IV

Experience, I have said, taught Verlaine nothing; religion had no more stable influence upon his conduct than experience. In that apology for himself which he wrote under the anagram of "Pauvre Lelian," he has stated the case with his usual sincerity. "I believe," he says, "and I sin in thought as in action; I believe, and I repent in thought, if no more. Or again, I believe, and I am a good Christian at this moment; I believe, and I am a bad Christian the instant after. The remembrance, the hope, the invocation of a sin delights me, with or without remorse, sometimes under the very form of sin, and hedged with all its natural consequences; more often— so strong, so natural and *animal,* are flesh and blood— just in the same manner as the remembrances, hopes, invocations of any carnal freethinker. This delight, I, you, some one else, writers, it pleases us to put to paper and publish more or less well expressed: we consign it, in short, into literary form, forgetting all religious ideas, or not letting one of them escape us. Can any one in good faith condemn us as poet? A hundred times no." And, indeed, I would echo, a hundred times no! It is just this apparent complication of what is really a great simplicity which gives its singular value to the poetry of Verlaine, permitting it to sum up in itself the whole paradox of humanity, and especially the weak, passionate, uncertain, troubled century to which we belong, in which so many doubts, negations, and distresses seem, now more than ever, to be struggling towards at least an ideal of spiritual consolation. Verlaine is the poet of these weaknesses and of that ideal.

JULES LAFORGUE

Jules Laforgue was born at Montevideo, of Breton parents, August 20, 1860. He died in Paris in 1887, two days before his twenty-seventh birthday. From 1880 to 1886 he had been reader to the Empress Augusta at Berlin. He married only a few months before his death. *D'allures?* says M. Gustave Kahn, *fort correctes, de hauts gibus, des cravates sobres, des vestons anglais, des pardessus clergymans, et de par les nécessités, un parapluie immuablement placé sous le bras.* His portraits show us a clean-shaved, reticent face, betraying little. With such a personality anecdotes have but small chance of appropriating those details by which expansive natures express themselves to the world. We know nothing about Laforgue which his work is not better able to tell us, even now that we have all his notes, unfinished fragments, and the letters of an almost virginal *naïveté* which he wrote to the woman whom he was going to marry. His entire work, apart from these additions, is contained in two small volumes, one of prose, the *Moralités Légendaires,* the other of verse, *Les Complaintes, L'Imitation de Notre-dame la Lune,* and a few other pieces, all published during the last three years of his life.

The prose and verse of Laforgue, scrupulously correct, but with a new manner of correctness, owe more than any one has realised to the half-unconscious prose and verse of Rimbaud. Verse and prose are alike a kind of travesty, making subtle use of colloquialism, slang, neologism, technical terms, for their allusive, their factitious, their reflected meanings, with which one can play, very seriously. The verse is alert, troubled, swaying, deliberately uncertain, hating rhetoric so piously that it prefers, and finds its piquancy in, the ridiculously obvious. It is really *vers libre,* but at the same time correct

verse, before *vers libre* had been invented. And it carries, as far as that theory has ever been carried, the
theory which demands an instantaneous notation (Whistler, let us say) of the figure or landscape which one has
been accustomed to define with such rigorous exactitude.
Verse, always elegant, is broken up into a kind of
mockery of prose.

> Encore un de mes pierrots mort;
> Mort d'un chronique orphelinisme;
> C'était un cœur plein de dandysme
> Lunaire, en un drôle de corps;

he will say to us, with a familiarity of manner, as of one
talking languidly, in a low voice, the lips always teased
into a slightly bitter smile; and he will pass suddenly
into the ironical lilt of

> Hôtel garni
> De l'infini,
> Sphinx et Joconde
> Des défunts mondes;

and from that into this solemn and smiling end of one of
his last poems, his own epitaph, if you will:

> Il prit froid l'autre automne,
> S'étant attardi vers les peines des cors,
> Sur la fin d'un beau jour.
> Oh! ce fut pour vos cors, et ce fut pour l'automne,
> Qu'il nous montra qu' "on meurt d'amour!"
> On ne le verra plus aux fêtes nationales,
> S'enfermer dans l'Histoire et tirer les verrous,
> Il vint trop tard, il est reparti sans scandale;
> O vous qui m'écoutez, rentrez chacun chez vous.

The old cadences, the old eloquence, the ingenuous seriousness of poetry, are all banished, on a theory as self-
denying as that which permitted Degas to dispense with
recognisable beauty in his figures. Here, if ever, is
modern verse, verse which dispenses with so many of the
privileges of poetry, for an ideal quite of its own. It is

after all, a very self-conscious ideal, becoming artificial through its extreme naturalness; for in poetry it is not "natural" to say things quite so much in the manner of the moment, with however ironical an intention.

The prose of the *Moralités Légendaires* is perhaps even more of a discovery. Finding its origin, as I have pointed out, in the experimental prose of Rimbaud, it carries that manner to a singular perfection. Disarticulated, abstract, mathematically lyrical, it gives expression, in its icy ecstasy, to a very subtle criticism of the universe, with a surprising irony of cosmical vision. We learn from books of mediæval magic that the embraces of the devil are of a coldness so intense that it may be called, by an allowable figure of speech, fiery. Everything may be as strongly its opposite as itself, and that is why this balanced, chill, colloquial style of Laforgue has, in the paradox of its intensity, the essential heat of the most obviously emotional prose. The prose is more patient than the verse, with its more compassionate laughter at universal experience. It can laugh as seriously, as profoundly, as in that graveyard monologue of Hamlet, Laforgue's Hamlet, who, Maeterlinck ventures to say, "is at moments more Hamlet than the Hamlet of Shakespeare." Let me translate a few sentences from it.

"Perhaps I have still twenty or thirty years to live, and I shall pass that way like the others. Like the others? O Totality, the misery of being there no longer! Ah! I would like to set out to-morrow, and search all through the world for the most adamantine processes of embalming. They, too, were, the little people of History, learning to read, trimming their nails, lighting the dirty lamp every evening, in love, gluttonous, vain, fond of compliments, hand-shakes, and kisses, living on bell-tower gossip, saying, 'What sort of weather shall we have to-morrow? Winter has really come. . . . We have had no plums this year.' Ah! everything is good, if it would not come to an end. And thou, Silence, pardon the Earth; the little madcap hardly knows what she is doing; on

the day of the great summing-up of consciousness before
the Ideal, she will be labelled with a pitiful *idem* in the
column of the miniature evolutions of the Unique Evo-
lution, in the column of negligible quantities . . . To
die! Evidently, one dies without knowing it, as, every
night, one enters upon sleep. One has no consciousness
of the passing of the last lucid thought into sleep, into
swooning, into death. Evidently. But to be no more,
to be here no more, to be ours no more! Not even to be
able, any more, to press against one's human heart, some
idle afternoon, the ancient sadness contained in one
little chord on the piano!"

In these always "lunar" parodies, *Salomé, Lohengrin,
Fils de Parsifal, Persée et Andromède,* each a kind of
metaphysical myth, he realises that *la créature va hardi-
ment à être cérébrale, anti-naturelle,* and he has invented
these fantastic puppets with an almost Japanese art of
spiritual dislocation. They are, in part, a way of taking
one's revenge upon science, by an ironical borrowing
of its very terms, which dance in his prose and verse,
derisively, at the end of a string.

In his acceptance of the fragility of things as actually
a principle of art, Laforgue is a sort of transformed
Watteau, showing his disdain for the world which fas-
cinates him, in quite a different way. He has constructed
his own world, lunar and actual, speaking slang and
astronomy, with a constant disengaging of the visionary
aspect, under which frivolity becomes an escape from
the arrogance of a still more temporary mode of being,
the world as it appears to the sober majority. He is
terribly conscious of daily life, cannot omit, mentally, a
single hour of the day; and his flight to the moon is in
sheer desperation. He sees what he calls *l'Inconscient* in
every gesture, but he cannot see it without these gestures.
And he sees, not only as an imposition, but a conquest,
the possibilities for art which come from the sickly
modern being, with his clothes, his nerves: the mere fact
that he flowers from the soil of his epoch.

It is an art of the nerves, this art of Laforgue, and it is what all art would tend towards if we followed our nerves on all their journeys. There is in it all the restlessness of modern life, the haste to escape from whatever weighs too heavily on the liberty of the moment, that capricious liberty which demands only room enough to hurry itself weary. It is distressingly conscious of the unhappiness of mortality, but it plays, somewhat uneasily, at a disdainful indifference. And it is out of these elements of caprice, fear, contempt, linked together by an embracing laughter, that it makes its existence.

Il n'y a pas de type, il y a la vie, Laforgue replies to those who come to him with classical ideals. *Votre idéal est bien vite magnifiquement submergé,* in life itself, which should form its own art, an art deliberately ephemeral, with the attaching pathos of passing things. There is a great pity at the root of this art of Laforgue: self-pity, which extends, with the artistic sympathy, through mere clearness of vision, across the world. His laughter, which Maeterlinck has defined so admirably as "the laughter of the soul," is the laughter of Pierrot, more than half a sob, and shaken out of him with a deplorable gesture of the thin arms, thrown wide. He is a metaphysical Pierrot, *Pierrot lunaire,* and it is of abstract notions, the whole science of the unconscious, that he makes his showman's patter. As it is part of his manner not to distinguish between irony and pity, or even belief, we need not attempt to do so. Heine should teach us to understand at least so much of a poet who could not otherwise resemble him less. In Laforgue, sentiment is squeezed out of the world before one begins to play at ball with it.

And so, of the two, he is the more hopeless. He has invented a new manner of being René or Werther: an inflexible politeness towards man, woman, and destiny. He composes love-poems hat in hand, and smiles with an exasperating tolerance before all the transformations of the eternal feminine. He is very conscious of death,

but his *blague* of death is, above all things, gentlemanly.
He will not permit himself, at any moment, the luxury
of dropping the mask: not at any moment.

Read this *Autre Complainte de Lord Pierrot,* with the
singular pity of its cruelty, before such an imagined
dropping of the mask:

> Celle qui doit me mettre au courant de la Femme!
>   Nous lui dirons d'abord, de mon air le moins froid:
> "La somme des angles d'un triangle, chère âme,
>   Est égale à deux droits."
>
> Et si ce cri lui part: "Dieu de Dieu que je t'aime!"
>   —"Dieu reconnaîtra les siens." Ou piquée au vif:
> —"Mes claviers ont du cœur, tu sera mon seul thème."
>   Moi: "Tout est relatif."
>
> De tous ses yeux, alors! se sentant trop banale:
>   "Ah! tu ne m'aime pas; tant d'autres sont jaloux!"
> Et moi, d'un œil qui vers l'Inconscient s'emballe:
>   "Merci, pas mal; et vous?"
>
> "Jouons au plus fidèle!"—A quoi bon, ô Nature!
>   "Autant à qui perd gagne." Alors, autre couplet:
> —"Ah! tu te lasseras le premier, j'en suis sûre."
>   —"Après vous, s'il vous plaît."
>
> Enfin, si, par un soir, elle meurt dans mes livres,
>   Douce; feignant de n'en pas croire encor mes yeux,
> J'aurai un: "Ah çà, mais, nous avions De Quoi vivre!
>   C'était donc sérieux?"

And yet one realises, if one but reads him attentively
enough, how much suffering and despair, and resignation
to what is, after all, the inevitable, are hidden away
under this disguise, and also why this disguise is possible.
Laforgue died at twenty-seven: he had been a dying man
all his life, and his work has the fatal evasiveness of those
who shrink from remembering the one thing which they
are unable to forget. Coming as he does after Rimbaud,
turning the divination of the other into theories, into
achieved results, he is the eternally grown up, mature to

the point of self-negation, as the other is the eternal *enfant terrible*. He thinks intensely about life, seeing what is automatic, pathetically ludicrous in it, almost as one might who has had no part in the comedy. He has the double advantage, for his art, of being condemned to death, and of being, in the admirable phrase of Villiers, "one of those who come into the world with a ray of moonlight in their brains."

STÉPHANE MALLARMÉ

I

STÉPHANE MALLARMÉ was one of those who love literature too much to write it except by fragments; in whom the desire of perfection brings its own defeat. With either more or less ambition he would have done more to achieve himself; he was always divided between an absolute aim at the absolute, that is, the unattainable, and a too logical disdain for the compromise by which, after all, literature is literature. Carry the theories of Mallarmé to a practical conclusion, multiply his powers in a direct ratio, and you have Wagner. It is his failure not to be Wagner. And, Wagner having existed, it was for him to be something more, to complete Wagner. Well, not being able to be that, it was a matter of sincere indifference to him whether he left one or two little, limited masterpieces of formal verse and prose, the more or the less. It was "the work" that he dreamed of, the new art, more than a new religion, whose precise form in the world he was never quite able to settle.

Un auteur difficile, in the phrase of M. Catulle Mendès, it has always been to what he himself calls "a labyrinth illuminated by flowers" that Mallarmé has felt it due to their own dignity to invite his readers. To their own dignity, and also to his. Mallarmé was obscure, not so much because he wrote differently, as because he thought differently, from other people. His mind was elliptical, and, relying with undue confidence on the intelligence of his readers, he emphasised the effect of what was unlike other people in his mind by resolutely ignoring even the links of connection that existed between them. Never having aimed at popularity, he never needed, as most writers need, to make the first advances. He made neither intrusion upon nor concession to those who, after all, were not obliged to read him. And when he spoke, he considered it neither needful nor seemly to listen in order to hear whether he was heard. To the charge of obscurity he replied, with sufficient disdain, that there are many who do not know how to read—except the newspaper, he adds, in one of those disconcerting, oddly-printed parentheses, which makes his work, to those who rightly apprehend it, so full of wise limitations, so safe from hasty or seemingly final conclusions. No one in our time has more significantly vindicated the supreme right of the artist in the aristocracy of letters; wilfully, perhaps, not always wisely, but nobly, logically. Has not every artist shrunk from that making of himself "a motley to the view," that handing over of his naked soul to the laughter of the multitude? But who, in our time, has wrought so subtle a veil, shining on this side, where the few are, a thick cloud on the other, where are the many? The oracles have always had the wisdom to hide their secrets in the obscurity of many meanings, or of what has seemed meaningless; and might it not, after all, be the finest epitaph for a self-respecting man of letters to be able to say, even after the writing of many books: I have kept my secret, I have not betrayed myself to the multitude?

But to Mallarmé, certainly, there might be applied the significant warning of Rossetti:

> Yet woe to thee if once thou yield
> Unto the act of doing nought!

After a life of persistent devotion to literature, he has

left enough poems to make a single small volume (less, certainly, than a hundred poems in all), a single volume of prose, a few pamphlets, and a prose translation of the poems of Poe. It is because among these there are masterpieces, poems which are among the most beautiful poems written in our time, prose which has all the subtlest qualities of prose, that, quitting the abstract point of view, we are forced to regret the fatal enchantments, fatal for him, of theories which are so greatly needed by others, so valuable for our instruction, if we are only a little careful in putting them into practice.

In estimating the significance of Stéphane Mallarmé, it is necessary to take into account not only his verse and prose, but, almost more than these, the Tuesdays of the Rue de Rome, in which he gave himself freely to more than one generation. No one who has ever climbed those four flights of stairs will have forgotten the narrow, homely interior, elegant with a sort of scrupulous Dutch comfort; the heavy, carved furniture, the tall clock, the portraits, Manet's, Whistler's, on the walls; the table on which the china bowl, odorous with tobacco, was pushed from hand to hand; above all, the rocking-chair, Mallarmé's, from which he would rise quietly, to stand leaning his elbow on the mantelpiece, while one hand, the hand which did not hold the cigarette, would sketch out one of those familiar gestures: *un peu de prêtre, un peu de danseuse* (in M. Rodenbach's admirable phrase), *avec lesquels il avait l'air chaque fois d'*entrer *dans la conversation, comme on entre en scène.* One of the best talkers of our time, he was, unlike most other fine talkers, harmonious with his own theories in giving no monologues, in allowing every liberty to his guests, to the conversation; in his perfect readiness to follow the slightest indication, to embroider upon any frame, with any material presented to him. There would have been something almost of the challenge of the improvisatore in this easily moved alertness of mental attitude, had it not been for the singular gentleness with which Mallarmé's

ecstasy, arrested in mid-flight. This ecstasy is never the mere instinctive cry of the heart, the simple human joy or sorrow, which, like the Parnassians, but for not quite the same reason, he did not admit in poetry. It is a mental transposition of emotion or sensation, veiled with atmosphere, and becoming, as it becomes a poem, pure beauty. Here, for instance, in a poem which I have translated line for line, and almost word for word, a delicate emotion, a figure vaguely divined, a landscape magically evoked, blend in a single effect.

SIGH

My soul, calm sister, towards thy brow, whereon scarce grieves
An autumn strewn already with its russet leaves,
And towards the wandering sky of thine angelic eyes,
Mounts, as in melancholy gardens may arise
Some faithful fountain sighing whitely towards the blue!
—Towards the blue pale and pure that sad October knew,
When, in those depths, it mirrored languors infinite,
And agonising leaves upon the waters white,
Windily drifting, traced a furrow cold and dun,
Where, in one long last ray, lingered the yellow sun.

Another poem comes a little closer to nature, but with what exquisite precautions, and with what surprising novelty in its unhesitating touch on actual things!

SEA-WIND

The flesh is sad, alas! and all the books are read.
Flight, only flight! I feel that birds are wild to tread
The floor of unknown foam, and to attain the skies!
Nought, neither ancient gardens mirrored in the eyes,
Shall hold this heart that bathes in waters its delight,
O nights! nor yet my waking lamp, whose lonely light
Shadows the vacant paper, whiteness profits best,
Nor the young wife who rocks her baby on her breast.
I will depart. O steamer, swaying rope and spar,
Lift anchor for exotic lands that lie afar!
A weariness, outworn by cruel hopes, still clings
To the last farewell handerchief's last beckonings!
And are not these, the masts inviting storms, not these

That an awakening wind bends over wrecking seas,
Lost, not a sail, a sail, a flowering isle, ere long?
But, O my heart, hear thou, hear thou the sailors' song!

These (need I say?) belong to the earlier period, in which Mallarmé had not yet withdrawn his light into the cloud; and to the same period belong the prose-poems, one of which, perhaps the most exquisite, I will translate here.

AUTUMN LAMENT

"Ever since Maria left me, for another star—which? Orion, Altair, or thou, green Venus?—I have always cherished solitude. How many long days I have passed, alone with my cat! By *alone,* I mean without a material being, and my cat is a mystical companion, a spirit. I may say, then, that I have passed long days alone with my cat, and alone, with one of the last writers of the Roman decadence; for since the white creature is no more, strangely and singularly, I have loved all that may be summed up in the word: fall. Thus, in the year, my favourite season is during those last languid summer days which come just before the autumn; and, in the day, the hour when I take my walk is the hour when the sun lingers before fading, with rays of copper-yellow on the grey walls, and of copper-red on the window-panes. And, just so, the literature from which my soul demands delight must be the poetry dying out of the last moments of Rome, provided, nevertheless, that it breathes nothing of the rejuvenating approach of the Barbarians, and does not stammer the infantile Latin of the first Christian prose.

"I read, then, one of those beloved poems (whose streaks of rouge have more charm for me than the fresh cheek of youth), and buried my hand in the fur of the pure animal, when a barrel-organ began to sing, languishingly and melancholy, under my window. It played in the long alley of poplars, whose leaves seem mourn-

ful to me even in spring, since Maria passed that way
with the tapers, for the last time. Yes, sad people's
instrument, truly: the piano glitters, the violin brings
one's torn fibres to the light, but the barrel-organ, in the
twilight of memory, has set me despairingly dreaming.
While it murmured a gaily vulgar air, such as puts mirth
into the heart of the suburbs, an old-fashioned, an empty
air, how came it that its refrain went to my very soul, and
made me weep like a romantic ballad? I drank it in, and
I did not throw a penny out of the window, for fear of
disturbing my own impression, and of perceiving that the
instrument was not singing by itself."

Between these characteristic, clear, and beautiful
poems, in verse and in prose, and the opaque darkness
of the later writings, come one or two poems, perhaps the
finest of all, in which already clearness is "a secondary
grace," but in which a subtle rapture finds incomparable
expression. *L'Après-midi d'un Faune* and *Hérodiade*
have already been introduced, in different ways, to
English readers: the former by Mr. Gosse, in a detailed
analysis; the latter by a translation into verse. And
Debussy, in his new music, has taken *L'Après-midi d'un
Faune* almost for his new point of departure, interpreting
it, at all events, faultlessly. In these two poems I find
Mallarmé at the moment when his own desire achieves
itself; when he attains Wagner's ideal, that "the most
complete work of the poet should be that which, in its
final achievement, becomes a perfect music": every word
is a jewel, scattering and recapturing sudden fire, every
image is a symbol, and the whole poem is visible music.
After this point began that fatal "last period" which
comes to most artists who have thought too curiously,
or dreamed too remote dreams, or followed a too wandering beauty. Mallarmé had long been too conscious that
all publication is "almost a speculation, on one's modesty,
for one's silence"; that "to unclench the fists, breaking
one's sedentary dream, for a ruffling face to face with the
idea," was after all unnecessary to his own conception of

himself, a mere way of convincing the public that one exists; and having achieved, as he thought, "the right to abstain from doing anything exceptional," he devoted himself, doubly, to silence. Seldom condescending to write, he wrote now only for himself, and in a manner which certainly saved him from intrusion. Some of Meredith's poems, and occasional passages of his prose, can alone give in English some faint idea of the later prose and verse of Mallarmé. The verse could not, I think, be translated; of the prose, in which an extreme lucidity of thought comes to us but glimmeringly through the entanglements of a construction, part Latin, part English, I shall endeavour to translate some fragments, in speaking of the theoretic writings, contained in the two volumes of *Vers et Prose* and *Divagations*.

III

It is the distinction of Mallarmé to have aspired after an impossible liberation of the soul of literature from what is fretting and constraining in "the body of that death," which is the mere literature of words. Words, he has realised, are of value only as a notation of the free breath of the spirit; words, therefore, must be employed with an extreme care, in their choice and adjustment, in setting them to reflect and chime upon one another; yet least of all for their own sake, for what they can never, except by suggestion, express. "Every soul is a melody," he has said, "which needs to be readjusted; and for that are the flute or viol of each." The word, treated indeed with a kind of "adoration," as he says, is so regarded in a magnificent sense, in which it is apprehended as a living thing, itself the vision rather than the reality; at least the philtre of the evocation. The word, chosen as he chooses it, is for him a liberating principle, by which the spirit is extracted from matter; takes form, perhaps assumes immortality. Thus an artificiality, even, in the use of words, that seeming artificiality which comes from using

words as if they had never been used before, that
chimerical search after the virginity of language, is but
the paradoxical outward sign of an extreme discontent
with even the best of their service. Writers who use words
fluently, seeming to disregard their importance, do so
from an unconscious confidence in their expressiveness,
which the scrupulous thinker, the precise dreamer, can
never place in the most carefully chosen among them. To
evoke, by some elaborate, instantaneous magic of language, without the formality of an after all impossible
description; to be, rather than to express: that is what
Mallarmé has consistently, and from the first, sought in
verse and prose. And he has sought this wandering, illusive, beckoning butterfly, the soul of dreams, over more
and more entangled ground; and it has led him into the
depths of many forests, far from the sunlight. To say that
he has found what he sought is impossible; but (is it
possible to avoid saying?) how heroic a search, and what
marvellous discoveries by the way!

I think I understand, though I cannot claim his own
authority for my supposition, the way in which Mallarmé
wrote verse, and the reason why it became more and more
abstruse, more and more unintelligible. Remember his
principle: that to name is to destroy, to suggest is to
create. Note, further, that he condemns the inclusion
in verse of anything but, "for example, the horror of the
forest, or the silent thunder afloat in the leaves; not the
intrinsic, dense wood of the trees." He has received,
then, a mental sensation: let it be the horror of the forest.
This sensation begins to form in his brain, at first probably no more than a rhythm, absolutely without words.
Gradually thought begins to concentrate itself (but with
an extreme care, lest it should break the tension on which
all depends) upon the sensation, already struggling to
find its own consciousness. Delicately, stealthily, with
infinitely timid precaution, words present themselves, at
first in silence. Every word seems like a desecration,
seems, the clearer it is, to throw back the original sensa-

tion farther and farther into the darkness. But, guided always by the rhythm, which is the executive soul (as, in Aristotle's definition, the soul is the form of the body), words come slowly, one by one, shaping the message. Imagine the poem already written down, at least composed. In its very imperfection, it is clear, it shows the links by which it has been riveted together; the whole process of its construction can be studied. Now most writers would be content; but with Mallarmé the work has only begun. In the final result there must be no sign of the making, there must be only the thing made. He works over it, word by word, changing a word here, for its colour, which is not precisely the colour required, a word there, for the break it makes in the music. A new image occurs to him, rarer, subtler, than the one he has used; the image is transferred. By the time the poem has reached, as it seems to him, a flawless unity, the steps of the progress have been only too effectually effaced; and while the poet, who has seen the thing from the beginning, still sees the relation of point to point, the reader, who comes to it only in its final stage, finds himself in a not unnatural bewilderment. Pursue this manner of writing to its ultimate development; start with an enigma, and then withdraw the key of the enigma; and you arrive, easily, at the frozen impenetrability of those latest sonnets, in which the absence of all punctuation is scarcely a recognisable hindrance.

That, I fancy to myself, was his actual way of writing; here, in what I prefer to give as a corollary, is the theory. "Symbolist, Decadent, or Mystic, the schools thus called by themselves, or thus hastily labelled by our information-press, adopt, for meeting-place, the point of an Idealism which (similarly as in fugues, in sonatas) rejects the 'natural' materials, and, as brutal, a direct thought ordering them; to retain no more than suggestion. To be instituted, a relation between images, exact; and that therefrom should detach itself a third aspect, fusible and clear, offered to the divination. Abolished, the pretension, æsthetically an error, despite its dominion over almost all the masterpieces, to enclose within the subtle paper other than, for example, the horror of the forest, or the silent thunder afloat in the leaves; not the intrinsic, dense wood of the trees. Some few bursts of personal pride, veridically trumpeted, awaken the architecture of the palace, alone habitable; not of stone, on which the pages would close but ill." For example (it is his own): "I say: a flower! and out of the oblivion to which my voice consigns every contour, so far as anything save the known calyx, musically arises, idea, and exquisite, the one flower absent from all bouquets." "The pure work," then, "implies the elocutionary disappearance of the poet, who yields place to the words, immobilised by the shock of their inequality; they take light from mutual reflection, like an actual train of fire over precious stones, replacing the old lyric afflatus or the enthusiastic personal direction of the phrase." "The verse which out of many vocables remakes an entire word, new, unknown to the language, and as if magical, attains this isolation of speech." Whence, it being "music which rejoins verse, to form, since Wagner, Poetry," the final conclusion: "That we are now precisely at the moment of seeking, before that breaking up of the large rhythms of literature, and their scattering in articulate, almost instrumental, nervous waves, an art which shall complete the transposition, into the Book, of the symphony, or simply recapture our own: for, it is not in elementary sonorities of brass, strings, wood, unquestionably, but in the intellectual word at its utmost, that, fully and evidently, we should find, drawing to itself all the correspondences of the universe, the supreme Music."

Here, literally translated, in exactly the arrangement of the original, are some passages out of the theoretic writings, which I have brought together, to indicate what seem to me the main lines of Mallarmé's doctrine. It is the doctrine which, as I have already said, had been divined by Gérard de Nerval; but what, in Gérard, was pure vision, becomes in Mallarmé a logical sequence of meditation. Mallarmé was not a mystic, to whom anything came unconsciously; he was a thinker, in whom an extraordinary subtlety of mind was exercised on always explicit, though by no means the common, problems. "A seeker after something in the world, that is there in no satisfying measure, or not at all," he pursued his search with unwearying persistence, with a sharp mental division of dream and idea, certainly very lucid to himself, however he may have failed to render his expression clear to others. And I, for one, cannot doubt that he was, for the most part, entirely right in his statement and analysis of the new conditions under which we are now privileged or condemned to write. His obscurity was partly his failure to carry out the spirit of his own directions; but, apart from obscurity, which we may all be fortunate enought to escape, is it possible for a writer, at the present day, to be quite simple, with the old, objective simplicity, in either thought or expression? To be *naïf*, to be archaic, is not to be either natural or simple; I affirm that it is not natural to be what is called "natural" any longer. We have no longer the mental attitude of those to whom a story was but a story, and all stories good; we have realised, since it was proved to us by Poe, not merely that the age of epics is past, but that no long poem was ever written; the finest long poem in the world being but a series of short poems linked together by prose. And, naturally, we can no longer write what we can no longer accept. Symbolism, implicit in all literature from the beginning, as it is implicit in the very words we use, comes to us now, at last quite conscious of itself, offering us the only escape from our many imprisonments. We find a new, an older, sense in the so worn out forms of things; the world, which we can no longer believe in as the satisfying material object it was to our grandparents, becomes transfigured with a new light; words, which long usage had darkened almost out of recognition, take fresh lustre. And it is on the

lines of that spritualising of the word, that perfecting of
form in its capacity for allusion and suggestion, that confidence in the eternal correspondences between the visible
and the invisible universe, which Mallarmé taught, and
too intermittently practised, that literature must now
move, if it is in any sense to move forward.

THE LATER HUYSMANS

IN the preface to his first novel, *Marthe: histoire d'une
fille,* thirty years ago, Huysmans defined his theory of art
in this defiant phrase: "I write what I see, what I feel,
and what I have experienced, and I write it as well as I
can: that is all." Ten or twelve years ago, he could still
say, in answer to an interviewer who asked him his
opinion of Naturalism: "At bottom, there are writers
who have talent and others who have not; let them be
Naturalists, Romantics, Decadents, what you will, it is
all the same to me: I only want to know if they have
talent." Such theoretical liberality, in a writer of original
talent, is a little disconcerting: it means that he is without a theory of his own, that he is not yet conscious of
having chosen his own way. And, indeed, it is only with
En Route that Huysmans can be said to have discovered
the direction in which he had really been travelling from
the beginning.

In a preface written not long since for a limited edition
of *À Rebours,* Huysmans confessed that he had never
been conscious of the direction in which he was travelling.
"My life and my literature," he affirmed, "have undoubtedly a certain amount of passivity, of the incalculable, of a direction not mine. I have simply obeyed; I
have been led by what are called 'mysterious ways.'"
He is speaking of the conversion which took him to
La Trappe in 1892, but the words apply to the whole
course of his career as a man of letters. In *Là-Bas,* which
is a sort of false start, he had, indeed, realised, though

for himself, at that time, ineffectually, that "it is essential
to preserve the veracity of the document, the precision
of detail, the fibrous and nervous language of Realism,
but it is equally essential to become the well-digger of
the soul, and not to attempt to explain what is mysterious
by mental maladies. . . . It is essential, in a word, to
follow the great road so deeply dug out by Zola, but it is
necessary also to trace a parallel pathway in the air, and
to grapple with the within and the after, to create, in a
word, a spiritual Naturalism." This is almost a definition
of the art of *En Route,* where this spiritual realism is
applied to the history of a soul, a conscience; in *La
Cathédrale* the method has still further developed, and
Huysmans becomes, in his own way, a Symbolist.

To the student of psychology few more interesting
cases could be presented than the development of Huysmans. From the first he has been a man "for whom the
visible world existed," indeed, but as the scene of a slow
martyrdom. The world has always appeared to him to
be a profoundly uncomfortable, unpleasant, and ridiculous place; and it has been a necessity of his temperament
to examine it minutely, with all the patience of disgust,
and a necessity of his method to record it with an almost
ecstatic hatred. In his first book, *Le Drageoir à Epices,*
published at the age of twenty-six, we find him seeking
his colour by preference in a drunkard's cheek or a
carcase outside a butcher's shop. *Marthe,* published at
Brussels in 1876, anticipates *La Fille Elisa* and *Nana,* but
it has a crude brutality of observation in which there is
hardly a touch of pity. *Les Sœurs Vatard* is a frame without a picture, but in *En Ménage* the dreary tedium of
existence is chronicled in all its insignificance with a
kind of weary and aching hate. "We, too," is its conclusion, "by leave of the everlasting stupidity of things,
may, like our fellow-citizens, live stupid and respected."
The fantastic unreality, the exquisite artificiality of *À
Rebours,* the breviary of the decadence, is the first sign
of that possible escape which Huysmans has always fore-

seen in the direction of art, but which he is still unable
to make into more than an artificial paradise, in which
beauty turns to a cruel hallucination and imprisons the
soul still more fatally. The end is a cry of hopeless hope,
in which Huysmans did not understand the meaning
till later: "Lord, have pity of the Christian who doubts,
of the sceptic who would fain believe, of the convict of
life who sets sail alone by night, under a firmament
lighted only by the consoling watch-lights of the old
hope."

In *Là-Bas* we are in yet another stage of this strange
pilgrim's progress. The disgust which once manifested
itself in the merely external revolt against the ugliness of
streets, the imbecility of faces, has become more and more
internalised, and the attraction of what is perverse in the
unusual beauty of art has led, by some obscure route, to
the perilous halfway house of a corrupt mysticism. The
book, with its monstrous pictures of the Black Mass and
of the spiritual abominations of Satanism, is one step
further in the direction of the supernatural; and this, too,
has its desperate, unlooked-for conclusion: "Christian
glory is a laughing-stock to our age; it contaminates the
supernatural and casts out the world to come." In *Là-
Bas* we go down into the deepest gulf; *En Route* sets us
one stage along a new way, and at this turning-point
begins the later Huysmans.

The old conception of the novel as an amusing tale of
adventures, though it has still its apologists in England,
has long since ceased in France to mean anything more
actual than powdered wigs and lace ruffles. Like children
who cry to their elders for "a story, a story," the English
public still wants its plot, its heroine, its villain. That
the novel should be psychological was a discovery as
early as Benjamin Constant, whose *Adolphe* anticipates
Le Rouge et le Noir, that rare, revealing, yet somewhat
arid masterpiece of Stendahl. But that psychology could
be carried so far into the darkness of the soul, that the
flaming walls of the world themselves faded to a glimmer,

was a discovery which had been made by no novelist before Huysmans wrote *En Route*. At once the novel showed itself capable of competing, on their own ground, with poetry, with the great "confessions," with philosophy. *En Route* is perhaps the first novel which does not set out with the aim of amusing its readers. It offers you no more entertainment than *Paradise Lost* or the *Confessions* of St. Augustine, and it is possible to consider it on the same level. The novel, which, after having chronicled the adventures of the Vanity Fairs of this world, has set itself with admirable success to analyse the amorous and ambitious and money-making intelligence of the conscious and practical self, sets itself at last to the final achievement: the revelation of the sub-conscious self, no longer the intelligence, but the soul. Here, then, purged of the distraction of incident, liberated from the bondage of a too realistic conversation, in which the aim had been to convey the very gesture of breathing life, internalised to a complete liberty, in which, just because it is so absolutely free, art is able to accept, without limiting itself, the expressive medium of a convention, we have in the novel a new form, which may be at once a confession and a decoration, the soul and a pattern.

This story of a conversion is a new thing in modern French; it is a confession, a self-ascultation of the soul; a kind of thinking aloud. It fixes, in precise words, all the uncertainties, the contradictions, the absurd unreasonableness and not less absurd logic, which distract man's brain in the passing over him of sensation and circumstance. And all this thinking is concentrated on one end, is concerned with the working out, in his own singular way, of one man's salvation. There is a certain dry hard casuistry, a subtlety and closeness almost ecclesiastical, in the investigation of an obscure and yet definite region, whose intellectual passions are as varied and as tumultuous as those of the heart. Every step is taken deliberately, is weighed, approved, condemned, viewed from this side and from that, and at the same time one feels behind all this reasoning an impulsion urging a soul onward against its will. In this astonishing passage, through Satanism to faith, in which the cry, "I am so weary of myself, so sick of my miserable existence," echoes through page after page, until despair dies into conviction, the conviction of "the uselessness of concerning oneself about anything but mysticism and the liturgy, of thinking about anything but about God," it is impossible not to see the sincerity of an actual, unique experience. The force of mere curiosity can go far, can penetrate to a certain depth; yet there is a point at which mere curiosity, even that of genius, comes to an end; and we are left to the individual soul's apprehension of what seems to it the reality of spiritual things. Such a personal apprehension comes to us out of this book, and at the same time, just as in the days when he forced language to express, in a more coloured and pictorial way than it had ever expressed before, the last escaping details of material things, so, in this analysis of the aberrations and warfares, the confessions and trials of the soul in penitence, Huysmans has found words for even the most subtle and illusive aspects of that inner life which he has come, at the last, to apprehend.

In *La Cathédrale* we are still occupied with this sensitive, lethargic, persevering soul, but with that soul in one of its longest halts by the way, as it undergoes the slow, permeating influence of *"la Cathédrale mystique par excellence,"* the cathedral of Chartres. And the greater part of the book is taken up with a study of this cathedral, of that elaborate and profound symbolism by which "the soul of sanctuaries" slowly reveals itself (*quel laconisme hermétique!*) with a sort of parallel interpretation of the symbolism which the Church of the Middle Ages concealed or revealed in colours, precious stones, plants, animals, numbers, odours, and in the Bible itself, in the setting together of the Old and New Testaments.

No doubt, to some extent this book is less interesting

than *En Route,* in the exact proportion in which everything in the world is less interesting than the human
soul. There are times when Durtal is almost forgotten,
and, unjustly enough, it may seem as if we are given this
archæology, these bestiaries, for their own sake. To fall
into this error is to mistake the whole purpose of the
book, the whole extent of the discovery in art which
Huysmans has been one of the first to make.

For in *La Cathédrale* Huysmans does but carry further
the principle which he had perceived in *En Route,* showing, as he does, how inert matter, the art of stones, the
growth of plants, the unconscious life of beasts, may be
brought under the same law of the soul, may obtain,
through symbol, a spiritual existence. He is thus but
extending the domain of the soul while he may seem to
be limiting or ignoring it; and Durtal may well stand
aside for a moment, in at least the energy of contemplation, while he sees, with a new understanding, the
very sight of his eyes, the very stuff of his thoughts, taking
life before him, a life of the same substance as his own.
What is Symbolism if not an establishing of the links
which hold the world together, the affirmation of an
eternal, minute, intricate, almost invisible life, which
runs through the whole universe? Every age has its own
symbols; but a symbol once perfectly expressed, that
symbol remains, as Gothic architecture remains the very
soul of the Middle Ages. To get at that truth which is
all but the deepest meaning of beauty, to find that symbol
which is its most adequate expression, is in itself a kind
of creation; and that is what Huysmans does for us in
La Cathédrale. More and more he has put aside all the
profane and accessible and outward pomp of writing for
an inner and more severe beauty of perfect truth. He has
come to realise that truth can be reached and revealed
only by symbol. Hence, all that description, that heaping
up of detail, that passionately patient elaboration: all
means to an end, not, as you may hastily incline to think,
ends in themselves.

It is curious to observe how often an artist perfects a particular means of expression long before he has any notion of what to do with it. Huysmans began by acquiring so astonishing a mastery of description that he could describe the inside of a cow hanging in a butcher's shop as beautifully as if it were a casket of jewels. The little work-girls of his early novels were taken for long walks, in which they would have seen nothing but the arm on which they lent and the milliners' shops which they passed; and what they did not see was described, marvellously, in twenty pages.

Huysmans is a brain all eye, a brain which sees even ideas as if they had a superficies. His style is always the same, whether he writes of a butcher's shop or of a stained-glass window; it is the immediate expression of a way of seeing, so minute and so intense that it becomes too emphatic for elegance and too coloured for atmosphere or composition, always ready to sacrifice euphony to either fact or colour. He cares only to give you the thing seen, exactly as he sees it, with all his love or hate, and with all the exaggeration which that feeling brings into it. And he loves beauty as a bulldog loves its mistress: by growling at all her enemies. He honours wisdom by annihilating stupidity. His art of painting in words resembles Monet's art of painting with his brush: there is the same power of rendering a vivid effect, almost deceptively, with a crude and yet sensitive realism. *"C'est pour la gourmandise de l'œil un gala de teintes,"* he says of the provision cellars at Hamburg; and this greed of the eye has eaten up in him almost every other sense. Even of music he writes as a deaf man with an eye for colour might write, to whom a musician had explained certain technical means of expression in music. No one has ever invented such barbarous and exact metaphors for the rendering of visual sensations. Properly, there is no metaphor; the words say exactly what they mean; they become figurative, as we call it, in their insistence on being themselves fact.

Huysmans knows that the motive force of the sentence lies in the verbs, and his verbs are the most singular, precise, and expressive in any language. But in subordinating, as he does, every quality to that of sharp, telling truth, the truth of extremes, his style loses charm; yet it can be dazzling; it has the solidity of those walls encrusted with gems which are to be seen in a certain chapel in Prague; it blazes with colour, and arabesques into a thousand fantastic patterns.

And now all that laboriously acquired mastery finds at last its use, lending itself to the new spirit with a wonderful docility. At last the idea which is beyond reality has been found, not where des Esseintes sought it, and a new meaning comes into what had once been scarcely more than patient and wrathful observation. The idea is there, visible, in his cathedral, like the sun which flashes into unity, into meaning, into intelligible beauty, the bewildering lozenges of colour, the inextricable trails of lead, which go to make up the picture in one of its painted windows. What, for instance, could be more precise in its translation of the different aspects under which the cathedral of Chartres can be seen, merely as colour, than this one sentence: "Seen as a whole, under a clear sky, its grey silvers, and, if the sun shines upon it, turns pale yellow and then golden; seen close, its skin is like that of a nibbled biscuit, with its silicious limestone eaten into holes; sometimes, when the sun is setting, it turns crimson, and rises up like a monstrous and delicate shrine, rose and green; and, at twilight, turns blue, then seems to evaporate as it fades into violet." Or, again, in a passage which comes nearer to the conventional idea of eloquence, how absolute an avoidance of a conventional phrase, a word used for its merely oratorical value: "High up, in space, like salamanders, human beings, with burning faces and flaming robes, lived in a firmament of fire; but these conflagrations were circumscribed, limited by an incombustible frame of darker glass, which beat back the clear young joy of the flames; by that kind of melancholy, that more serious and more aged aspect, which is taken by the duller colours. The hue and cry of reds, the limpid security of whites, the reiterated halleluias of yellows, the virginal glory of blues, all the quivering hearth-glow of painted glass, dies away as it came near this border coloured with the rust of iron, with the russet of sauce, with the harsh violet of sandstone, with bottle-green, with the brown of touchwood, with sooty black, with ashen grey."

This, in its excess of exactitude (how mediæval a quality!) becomes, on one page, a comparison of the tower without a spire to an unsharpened pencil which cannot write the prayers of earth upon the sky. But for the most part it is a consistent humanising of too objectively visible things, a disengaging of the sentiment which exists in them, which is one of the secrets of their appeal to us, but which for the most part we overlook as we set ourselves to add up the shapes and colours which have enchanted us. To Huysmans this artistic discovery has come, perhaps in the most effectual way, but certainly in the way least probable in these days, through faith, a definite religious faith; so that, beginning tentatively, he has come, at last, to believe in the Catholic Church as a monk of the Middle Ages believed in it. And there is no doubt that to Huysmans this abandonment to religion has brought, among other gifts, a certain human charity in which he was notably lacking, removing at once one of his artistic limitations. It has softened his contempt of humanity; it has broadened his outlook on the world. And the sense, diffused through the whole of this book, of the living and beneficent reality of the Virgin, of her real presence in the cathedral built in her honour and after her own image, brings a strange and touching kind of poetry into these closely and soberly woven pages.

From this time forward, until his death, Huysmans is seen purging himself of his realism, coming closer and closer to that spiritual Naturalism which he had invented, an art made out of an apprehension of the inner

meaning of those things which he still saw with the old
tenacity of vision. Nothing is changed in him and yet
all is changed. The disgust of the world deepens through
L'Oblat, which is the last stage but one in the pilgrimage
which begins with *En Route.* It seeks an escape in por-
ing, with a dreadful diligence, over a saint's recorded
miracles, in the life of *Sainte Lydwine de Schiedam,*
which is mediæval in its precise acceptance of every
horrible detail of the story. *Les Foules de Lourdes* has
the same minute attentiveness to horror, but with a new
pity in it, and a way of giving thanks to the Virgin, which
is in Huysmans yet another escape from his disgust of the
world. But it is in the great chapter on Satan as the
creator of ugliness that his work seems to end where it
had begun, in the service of art, now come from a great
way off to join itself with the service of God. And the
whole soul of Huysmans characterises itself in the turn
of a single phrase there: that "art is the only clean thing
on earth, except holiness."

MAETERLINCK AS A MYSTIC

THE secret of things which is just beyond the most subtle
words, the secret of the expressive silences, has always
been clearer to Maeterlinck than to most people; and, in
his plays, he has elaborated an art of sensitive, taciturn,
and at the same time highly ornamental simplicity, which
has come nearer than any other art to being the voice
of silence. To Maeterlinck the theatre has been, for the
most part, no more than one of the disguises by which he
can express himself, and with his book of meditations on
the inner life, *Le Trésor des Humbles,* he may seem to
have dropped his disguise.

All art hates the vague; not the mysterious, but the
vague; two opposites very commonly confused, as the
secret with the obscure, the infinite with the indefinite.
And the artist who is also a mystic hates the vague with

a more profound hatred than any other artist. Thus Maeterlinck, endeavouring to clothe mystical conceptions in concrete form, has invented a drama so precise, so curt, so arbitrary in its limits, that it can safely be confided to the masks and feigned voices of marionettes. His theatre of artificial beings, who are at once more ghostly and more mechanical than the living actors whom we are accustomed to see, in so curious a parody of life, moving with a certain freedom of action across the stage, may be taken as itself a symbol of the aspect under which what we fantastically term "real life" presents itself to the mystic. Are we not all puppets, in a theatre of marionettes, in which the parts we play, the dresses we wear, the very emotion whose dominance gives its express form to our faces, have all been chosen for us; in which I, it may be, with curled hair and a Spanish cloak, play the romantic lover, sorely against my will, while you, a "fair penitent" for no repented sin, pass whitely under a nun's habit? And as our parts have been chosen for us, our motions controlled from behind the curtain, so the words we seem to speak are but spoken through us, and we do but utter fragments of some elaborate invention, planned for larger ends than our personal display or convenience, but to which, all the same, we are in a humble degree necessary. This symbolical theatre, its very existence being a symbol, has perplexed many minds, to some of whom it has seemed puerile, a child's mystification of small words and repetitions, a thing of attitudes and omissions; while others, yet more unwisely, have compared it with the violent, rhetorical, most human drama of the Elizabethans, with Shakespeare himself, to whom all the world was a stage, and the stage all this world, certainly. A sentence, already famous, of the *Trésor des Humbles,* will tell you what it signifies to Maeterlinck himself.

"I have come to believe," he writes, in *Le Tragique Quotidien,* "that an old man seated in his armchair, waiting quietly under the lamplight, listening without knowing it to all the eternal laws which reign about his house, interpreting without understanding it all that there is in the silence of doors and windows, and in the little voice of light, enduring the presence of his soul and of his destiny, bowing his head a little, without suspecting that all the powers of the earth intervene and stand on guard in the room like attentive servants, not knowing that the sun itself suspends above the abyss the little table on which he rests his elbow, and that there is not a star in the sky nor a force in the soul which is indifferent to the motion of a falling eyelid or a rising thought—I have come to believe that this motionless old man lived really a more profound, human, and universal life than the lover who strangles his mistress, the captain who gains a victory, or the husband who 'avenges his honour.' "

That, it seems to me, says all there is to be said of the intention of this drama which Maeterlinck has evoked; and, of its style, this other sentence, which I take from the same essay: "It is only the words that at first sight seem useless which really count in a work."

This drama, then, is a drama founded on philosophical ideas, apprehended emotionally; on the sense of the mystery of the universe, of the weakness of humanity, that sense which Pascal expressed when he said: *Ce qui m'étonne le plus est de voir que tout le monde n'est pas étonné de sa faiblesse;* with an acute feeling of the pathetic ignorance in which the souls nearest to one another look out upon their neighbours. It is a drama in which the interest is concentrated on vague people, who are little parts of the universal consciousness, their strange names being but the pseudonyms of obscure passions, intimate emotions. They have the fascination which we find in the eyes of certain pictures, so much more real and disquieting, so much more permanent with us, than living people. And they have the touching simplicity of children; they are always children in their ignorance of themselves, of one another, and of fate. And, because they are so disembodied of the more trivial accidents of life, they give themselves without limitation to whatever passionate instinct possesses them. I do not know a more passionate love-scene than that scene in the wood beside the fountain, where Pelléas and Mélisande confess the strange burden which has come upon them. When the soul gives itself absolutely to love, all the barriers of the world are burnt away, and all its wisdom and subtlety are as incense poured on a flame. Morality, too, is burnt away, no longer exists, any more than it does for children or for God.

Maeterlinck has realised, better than any one else, the significance, in life and art, of mystery. He has realised how unsearchable is the darkness out of which we have but just stepped, and the darkness into which we are about to pass. And he has realised how the thought and sense of that twofold darkness invade the little space of light in which, for a moment, we move; the depth to which they shadow our steps, even in that moment's partial escape. But in some of his plays he would seem to have apprehended this mystery as a thing merely or mainly terrifying; the actual physical darkness surrounding blind men, the actual physical approach of death as the intruder; he has shown us people huddled at a window, out of which they are almost afraid to look, or beating at a door, the opening of which they dread. Fear shivers through these plays, creeping across our nerves like a damp mist coiling up out of a valley. And there is beauty, certainly, in this "vague spiritual fear"; but a less obvious kind of beauty than that which gives its profound pathos to *Aglavaine et Sélysette,* the one play written since the writing of the essays. Here is mystery, which is also pure beauty, in these delicate approaches of intellectual pathos, in which suffering and death and error become transformed into something almost happy, so full is it of strange light.

And the aim of Maeterlinck, in his plays, is not only to render the soul and the soul's atmosphere, but to reveal

this strangeness, pity, and beauty through beautiful pictures. No dramatist has ever been so careful that his
scenes should be in themselves beautiful, or has made the
actual space of forest, tower, or seashore so emotionally
significant. He has realised, after Wagner, that the art
of the stage is the art of pictorial beauty, of the correspondence in rhythm between the speakers, their words,
and their surroundings. He has seen how, in this way,
and in this way alone, the emotion, which it is but a
part of the poetic drama to express, can be at once in-
tensified and purified

It is only after hinting at many of the things which he
had to say in these plays, which have, after all, been a
kind of subterfuge, that Maeterlinck has cared, or been
able, to speak with the direct utterance of the essays. And
what may seem curious is that this prose of the essays,
which is the prose of a doctrine, is incomparably more
beautiful than the prose of the plays, which was the prose
of an art. Holding on this point a different opinion
from one who was, in many senses, his master, Villiers de
l'Isle-Adam, he did not admit that beauty of words, or
even any expressed beauty of thoughts, had its place in
spoken dialogue, even though it was not two living actors
speaking to one another on the stage, but a soul speaking
to a soul, and imagined speaking through the mouths of
marionettes. But that beauty of phrase which makes the
profound and sometimes obscure pages of *Axël* shine
as with the crossing fire of jewels, rejoices us, though with
a softer, a more equable, radiance, in the pages of these
essays, in which every sentence has the indwelling beauty
of an intellectual emotion, preserved at the same height
of tranquil ecstasy from first page to last. There is a
sort of religious calm in these deliberate sentences, into
which the writer has known how to introduce that divine
monotony which is one of the accomplishments of great
style. Never has simplicity been more ornate or a fine
beauty more visible through its self-concealment.

But, after all, the claim upon us of this book is not the claim of a work of art, but of a doctrine, and more than that, of a system. Belonging, as he does, to the eternal hierarchy, the unbroken succession, of the mystics, Maeterlinck has apprehended what is essential in the mystical doctrine with a more profound comprehension, and thus more systematically, than any mystic of recent times. He has many points of resemblance with Emerson, on whom he has written an essay which is properly an exposition of his own personal ideas; but Emerson, who proclaimed the supreme guidance of the inner light, the supreme necessity of trusting instinct, of honouring emotion, did but proclaim all this, not without a certain antimystical vagueness: Maeterlinck has systematised it. A more profound mystic than Emerson, he has greater command of that which comes to him unawares, is less at the mercy of visiting angels.

Also, it may be said that he surrenders himself to them more absolutely, with less reserve and discretion; and, as he has infinite leisure, his contemplation being subject to no limits of time, he is ready to follow them on unknown rounds, to any distance, in any direction, ready also to rest in any wayside inn, without fearing that he will have lost the road on the morrow.

This old gospel, of which Maeterlinck is the new voice, has been quietly waiting until certain bankruptcies, the bankruptcy of Science, of the Positive Philosophies, should allow it full credit. Considering the length even of time, it has not had an unreasonable space of waiting; and remember that it takes time but little into account. We have seen many little gospels demanding of every emotion, of every instinct, "its certificate at the hand of some respectable authority." Without confidence in themselves or in things, and led by Science, which is as if one were led by one's notebook, they demand a reasonable explanation of every mystery. Not finding that explanation, they reject the mystery; which is as if the fly on the wheel rejected the wheel because it was hidden from his eyes by the dust of its own raising.

The mystic is at once the proudest and the humblest of men. He is as a child who resigns himself to the guidance of an unseen hand, the hand of one walking by his side; he resigns himself with the child's humility. And he has the pride of the humble, a pride manifesting itself in the calm rejection of every accepted map of the roads, of every offer of assistance, of every painted sign-post pointing out the smoothest ways on which to travel. He demands no authority for the unseen hand whose fingers he feels upon his wrist. He conceives of life, not, indeed, so much as a road on which one walks, very much at one's own discretion, but as a blown and wandering ship, surrounded by a sea from which there is no glimpse of land; and he conceives that to the currents of that sea he may safely trust himself. Let his hand, indeed, be on the rudder, there will be no miracle worked for him; it is enough miracle that the sea should be there, and the ship, and he himself. He will never know why his hand should turn the rudder this way rather than that.

Jacob Boehme has said, very subtly, "that man does not perceive the truth but God perceives the truth in man"; that is, that whatever we perceive or do is not perceived or done consciously by us, but unconsciously through us. Our business, then, is to tend that "inner light" by which most mystics have symbolised that which at once guides us in time and attaches us to eternity. This inner light is no miraculous descent of the Holy Spirit, but the perfectly natural, though it may finally be overcoming, ascent of the spirit within us. The spirit, in all men, being but a ray of the universal light, it can, by careful tending, by the removal of all obstruction, the cleansing of the vessel, the trimming of the wick, as it were, be increased, made to burn with a steadier, a brighter flame. In the last rapture it may become dazzling, may blind the watcher with excess of light, shutting him in within the circle of transfiguration, whose extreme radiance will leave all the rest of the world henceforth one darkness.

All mystics being concerned with what is divine in life, with the laws which apply equally to time and eternity, it may happen to one to concern himself chiefly with time seen under the aspect of eternity, to another to concern himself rather with eternity seen under the aspect of time. Thus many mystics have occupied themselves, very profitably, with showing how natural, how explicable on their own terms, are the mysteries of life; the whole aim of Maeterlinck is to show how mysterious all life is, "what an astonishing thing it is, merely to live." What he had pointed out to us, with certain solemn gestures, in his plays, he sets himself now to affirm, slowly, fully, with that "confidence in mystery" of which he speaks. Because "there is not an hour without its familiar miracles and its ineffable suggestions," he sets himself to show us these miracles and these meanings where others have not always sought or found them, in women, in children, in the theatre. He seems to touch, at one moment or another, whether he is discussing *La Beauté Intérieure* or *Le Tragique Quotidien,* on all of these hours, and there is no hour so dark that his touch does not illuminate it. And it is characteristic of him, of his "confidence in mystery," that he speaks always without raising his voice, without surprise or triumph, or the air of having said anything more than the simplest observation. He speaks, not as if he knew more than others, or had sought out more elaborate secrets, but as if he had listened more attentively.

Loving most those writers "whose works are nearest to silence," he begins his book, significantly, with an essay on Silence, an essay which, like all these essays, has the reserve, the expressive reticence, of those "active silences" of which he succeeds in revealing a few of the secrets.

"Souls," he tells us, "are weighed in silence, as gold and silver are weighed in pure water, and the words which we pronounce have no meaning except through the silence in which they are bathed. We seek to know that we may learn not to know"; knowledge, that which can be known by the pure reason, metaphysics, "indispensable" on this side of the "frontiers," being after all precisely what is least essential to us, since least essentially ourselves. "We possess a self more profound and more boundless than the self of the passions or of pure reason. . . . There comes a moment when the phenomena of our customary consciousness, what we may call the consciousness of the passions or of our normal relationships, no longer mean anything to us, no longer touch our real life. I admit that this consciousness is often interesting in its way, and that it is often necessary to know it thoroughly. But it is a surface plant, and its roots fear the great central fire of our being. I may commit a crime without the least breath stirring the tiniest flame of this fire; and, on the other hand, the crossing of a single glance, a thought which never comes into being, a minute which passes without the utterance of a word, may rouse it into terrible agitations in the depths of its retreat, and cause it to overflow upon my life. Our soul does not judge as we judge; it is a capricious and hidden thing. It can be reached by a breath and unconscious of a tempest. Let us find out what reaches it; everything is there, for it is there that we ourselves are."

And it is towards this point that all the words of this book tend. Maeterlinck, unlike most men ("What is man but a God who is afraid?"), is not "miserly of immortal things." He utters the most divine secrets without fear, betraying certain hiding-places of the soul in those most nearly inaccessible retreats which lie nearest to us. All that he says we know already; we may deny it, but we know it. It is what we are not often at leisure enough with ourselves, sincere enough with ourselves, to realise; what we often dare not realise; but, when he says it, we know that it is true, and our knowledge of it is his warrant for saying it. He is what he is precisely because he tells us nothing which we do not already know, or it may be, what we have known and forgotten.

The mystic, let it be remembered, has nothing in common with the moralist. He speaks only to those who are already prepared to listen to him, and he is indifferent to the "practical" effect which these or others may draw from his words. A young and profound mystic of our day has figured the influence of wise words upon the foolish and headstrong as "torches thrown into a burning city." The mystic knows well that it is not always the soul of the drunkard or the blasphemer which is farthest from the eternal beauty. He is concerned only with that soul of the soul, that life of life, with which the day's doings have so little to do; itself a mystery, and at home only among those supreme mysteries which surround it like an atmosphere. It is not always that he cares that his message, or his vision, may be as clear to others as it is to himself. But, because he is an artist, and not only a philosopher, Maeterlinck has taken especial pains that not a word of his may go astray, and there is not a word of this book which needs to be read twice, in order that it may be understood, by the least trained of attentive readers. It is, indeed, as he calls it, "The Treasure of the Lowly."

CONCLUSION

OUR only chance, in this world, of a complete happiness, lies in the measure of our success in shutting the eyes of the mind, and deadening its sense of hearing, and dulling the keenness of its apprehension of the unknown. Knowing so much less than nothing, for we are entrapped in smiling and many-coloured appearances, our life may seem to be but a little space of leisure, in which it will be the necessary business of each of us to speculate on what is so rapidly becoming the past and so rapidly becoming the future, that scarcely existing present which is after all our only possession. Yet, as the present passes from us, hardly to be enjoyed except as memory or as hope, and only with an at best partial recognition of the uncertainty or inutility of both, it is with a kind of terror that we wake up, every now and then, to the whole knowledge of our ignorance, and to some perception of where it is leading us. To live through a single day with that overpowering consciousness of our real position, which, in the moments in which alone it mercifully comes, is like blinding light or the thrust of a flaming sword, would drive any man out of his senses. It is our hesitations, the excuses of our hearts, the compromises of our intelligence, which save us. We can forget so much, we can bear suspense with so fortunate an evasion of its real issues; we are so admirably finite.

And so there is a great, silent conspiracy between us to forget death; all our lives are spent in busily forgetting death. That is why we are active about so many things which we know to be unimportant; why we are so afraid of solitude, and so thankful for the company of our fellow-creatures. Allowing ourselves, for the most part, to be but vaguely conscious of that great suspense in which we live, we find our escape from its sterile, annihilating reality in many dreams, in religion, passion, art; each a forgetfulness, each a symbol of creation; religion being the creation of a new heaven, passion the creation of a new earth, and art, in its mingling of heaven and earth, the creation of heaven out of earth. Each is a kind of sublime selfishness, the saint, the lover, and the artist having each an incommunicable ecstasy which he esteems as his ultimate attainment, however, in his lower moments, he may serve God in action, or do the will of his mistress, or minister to men by showing them a little beauty. But it is, before all things, an escape; and the prophets who have redeemed the world, and the artists who have made the world beautiful, and the lovers who have quickened the pulses of the world, have really, whether they knew it or not, been fleeing from the certainty of one thought: that we have, all of us, only our one day; and from the dread of that other thought: that the day, however used, must after all be wasted.

The fear of death is not cowardice; it is, rather, an intellectual dissatisfaction with an enigma which has been presented to us, and which can be solved only when its solution is of no further use. All we have to ask of death is the meaning of life, and we are waiting all through life to ask that question. That life should be happy or unhappy, as those words are used, means so very little; and the heightening or lessening of the general felicity of the world means so little to any individual. There is something almost vulgar in happiness which does not become joy, and joy is an ecstasy which can rarely be maintained in the soul for more than the moment during which we recognise that it is not sorrow. Only very young people want to be happy. What we all want is to be quite sure that there is something which makes it worth while to go on living, in what seems to us our best way, at our finest intensity; something beyond the mere fact that we are satisfying a sort of inner logic (which may be quite faulty) and that we get our best makeshift for happiness on that so hazardous assumption.

Well, the doctrine of Mysticism, with which all this symbolical literature has so much to do, of which it is all so much the expression, presents us, not with a guide for conduct, not with a plan for our happiness, not with an explanation of any mystery, but with a theory of life which makes us familiar with mystery, and which seems to harmonise those instincts which make for religion, passion, and art, freeing us at once of a great bondage. The final uncertainty remains, but we seem to knock less helplessly at closed doors, coming so much closer to the once terrifying eternity of things about us, as we come to look upon these things as shadows, through which we have our shadowy passage. "For in the particular acts of human life," Plotinus tells us, "it is not the interior soul and the true man, but the exterior shadow of the man alone, which laments and weeps, performing his part on the earth as in a more ample and extended scene, in which many shadows of souls and phantom scenes appear." And as we realise the identity of a poem, a prayer, or a kiss, in that spiritual universe which we are weaving for ourselves, each out of a thread of the great fabric; as we realise the infinite insignificance of action, its immense distance from the current of life; as we realise the delight of feeling ourselves carried onward by forces which it is our wisdom to obey; it is at least with a certain relief that we turn to an ancient doctrine, so much the more likely to be true because it has so much the air of a dream. On this theory alone does all life become worth living, all art worth making, all worship worth offering. And because it might slay as well as save, because the freedom of its sweet captivity might so easily become deadly to the fool, because that is the hardest path to walk in where you are told only, walk well; it is perhaps the only counsel of perfection which can ever really mean much to the artist.

ESSAYS

ADDED TO THE REVISED EDITION

OF 1919

BALZAC

I

THE first man who has completely understood Balzac is
Rodin, and it has taken Rodin ten years to realise his
own conception. France has refused the statue in which a
novelist is represented as a dreamer, to whom Paris is
not so much Paris as Patmos: "the most Parisian of our
novelists," Frenchmen assure you. It is more than a
hundred years since Balzac was born: a hundred years is
a long time in which to be misunderstood with admiration.

In choosing the name of the *Human Comedy* for a
series of novels in which, as he says, there is at once "the
history and the criticism of society, the analysis of its
evils, and the discussion of its principles," Balzac proposed to do for the modern world what Dante, in his
Divine Comedy, had done for the world of the Middle
Ages. Condemned to write in prose, and finding his
opportunity in that restriction, he created for himself a
form which is perhaps the nearest equivalent for the epic
or the poetic drama, and the only form in which, at all
events, the epic is now possible. The world of Dante
was materially simple compared with the world of the
nineteenth century; the "visible world" had not yet
begun to "exist," in its tyrannical modern sense; the
complications of the soul interested only the Schoolmen,
and were a part of theology; poetry could still represent
an age and yet be poetry. But to-day poetry can no longer
represent more than the soul of things; it had taken
refuge from the terrible improvements of civilisation in
a divine seclusion, where it sings, disregarding the many

voices of the street. Prose comes offering its infinite
capacity for detail; and it is by the infinity of its detail
that the novel, as Balzac created it, has become the
modern epic.

There had been great novels, indeed, before Balzac,
but no great novelist; and the novels themselves are
scarcely what we should to-day call by that name. The
interminable *Astrée* and its companions form a link between the *fabliaux* and the novel, and from them
developed the characteristic eighteenth-century *conte,* in
narrative, letters, or dialogue, as we see it in Marivaux,
Laclos, Crébillon *fils.* Crébillon's longer works, includ-
ing *Le Sopha,* with their conventional paraphernalia of
Eastern fable, are extremely tedious; but in two short
pieces, *La Nuit et le Moment* and *Le Hasard du Coin du
Feu,* he created a model of witty, naughty, deplorably
natural comedy, which to this day is one of the most characteristic French forms of fiction. Properly, however, it
is a form of the drama rather than of the novel. Laclos,
in *Les Liaisons Dangereuses,* a masterpiece which scandalised the society that adored Crébillon, because its
naked human truth left no room for sentimental excuses, comes much nearer to prefiguring the novel (as
Stendhal, for instance, is afterward to conceive it), but
still preserves the awkward traditional form of letters.
Marivaux had indeed already seemed to suggest the novel
of analysis, but in a style which has christened a whole
manner of writing that precisely which is least suited to
the writing of fiction. Voltaire's *contes, La Religieuse* of
Diderot, are tracts or satires in which the story is only
an excuse for the purpose. Rousseau, too, has his purpose,
even in *La Nouvelle Héloïse,* but it is a humanising
purpose; and with that book the novel of passion comes
into existence, and along with it the descriptive novel.
Yet with Rousseau this result is an accident of genius; we
cannot call him a novelist; and we find him abandoning
the form he has found, for another, more closely personal,
which suits him better. Restif de la Bretonne, who

followed Rousseau at a distance, not altogether wisely, developed the form of half-imaginary autobiography in *Monsieur Nicolas,* a book of which the most significant part may be compared with Hazlitt's *Liber Amoris.* Morbid and even mawkish as it is, it has a certain uneasy, unwholesome humanity in its confessions, which may seem to have set a fashion only too scrupulously followed by modern French novelists. Meanwhile, the Abbé Prévost's one great story, *Manon Lescaut,* had brought for once a purely objective study, of an incomparable simplicity, into the midst of these analyses of difficult souls; and then we return to the confession, in the works of others not novelists: Benjamin Constant, Mme. de Staël, Chateaubriand, in *Adolphe, Corinne, René.* At once we are in the Romantic movement, a movement which begins lyrically among poets, and at first with a curious disregard of the more human part of humanity.

Balzac worked contemporaneously with the Romantic movement, but he worked outside it, and its influence upon him is felt only in an occasional pseudo-romanticism, like the episode of the pirate in *La Femme de Trente Ans.* His vision of humanity was essentially a poetic vision, but he was a poet whose dreams were facts. Knowing that, as Mme. Necker has said, "the novel should be the better world," he knew also that "the novel would be nothing if, in that august lie, it were not true in details." And in the *Human Comedy* he proposed to himself to do for society more than Buffon had done for the animal world.

"There is but one animal," he declares, in his *Avant-Propos,* with a confidence which Darwin has not yet come to justify. But "there exists, there will always exist, social species, as there are zoological species. . . . Thus the work to be done will have a triple form: men, women, and things; that is to say, human beings and the material representation which they give to their thought; in short, man and life." And, studying after nature, "French

society will be the historian, I shall need to be no more
than the secretary." Thus will be written "the history
forgotten by so many historians, the history of manners."
But that is not all, for "passion is the whole of humanity. . . . In realizing clearly the drift of the composition, it will be seen that I assign to facts, constant, daily,
open, or secret, to the acts of individual life, to their
causes and principles, as much importance as historians
had formerly attached to the events of the public life
of nations. . . . Facts gathered together and painted as
they are, with passion for element," is one of his defini-
tions of the task he has undertaken. And in a letter to
Mme. de Hanska, he summarises every detail of his
scheme.

"The *Études des Mœurs* will represent social effects,
without a single situation of life, or a physiognomy, or
a character of man or woman, or a manner of life, or a
profession, or a social zone, or a district of France, or
anything pertaining to childhood, old age, or maturity,
politics, justice, or war, having been forgotten.

"That laid down, the history of the human heart
traced link by link, the history of society made in all its
details, we have the base. . . .

"Then, the second stage is the *Études philosophiques*,
for after the *effects* come the *causes*. In the *Études des
Mœurs* I shall have painted the sentiments and their
action, life and the fashion of life. In the *Études
philosophiques* I shall say *why the sentiments, on what
the life*. . . .

"Then, after the *effects* and the *causes*, come the *Études
analytiques*, to which the *Physiologie du mariage* belongs,
for, after the *effects* and the *causes*, one should seek the
principles. . . .

"After having done the poetry, the demonstration, of a
whole system, I shall do the science in the *Essai sur les
forces humaines*. And, on the bases of this palace I shall
have traced the immense arabesque of the *Cent Contes
drolatiques!*"

Quite all that, as we know, was not carried out; but there, in its intention, is the plan; and after twenty years' work the main part of it, certainly, was carried out. Stated with this precise detail, it has something of a scientific air, as of a too deliberate attempt upon the sources of life by one of those systematic French minds which are so much more logical than facts. But there is one little phrase to be noted: "La passion est toute l'humanité." All Balzac is in that phrase.

Another French novelist, following, as he thought, the example of the *Human Comedy,* has endeavoured to build up a history of his own time with even greater minuteness. But *Les Rougon-Macquart* is no more than system; Zola has never understood that detail without life is the wardrobe without the man. Trying to outdo Balzac on his own ground, he has made the fatal mistake of taking him only on his systematic side, which in Balzac is subordinate to a great creative intellect, an incessant, burning thought about men and women, a passionate human curiosity for which even his own system has no limits. "The misfortunes of the *Birotteaus,* the priest and the perfumer," he says, in his *Avant-Propos,* taking an example at random, "are, for me, those of humanity." To Balzac manners are but the vestment of life; it is life that he seeks; and life, to him (it is his own word) is but the vestment of thought. Thought is at the root of all his work, a whole system of thought, in which philosophy is but another form of poetry; and it is from this root of idea that the *Human Comedy* springs.

II

The two books into which Balzac has put his deepest thought, the two books which he himself cared for the most, are *Séraphita* and *Louis Lambert.* Of *Louis Lambert* he said: "I write it for myself and a few others"; of *Séraphita*: "My life is in it. . . . One could write *Goriot* any day," he adds; "*Séraphita* only once in a lifetime."

world like our own, but a world infinitely more vigorous, interesting, profound; more beautiful with that kind of beauty which nature finds of itself for art. It is the quality of great creative art to give us so much life that we are almost overpowered by it, as by an air almost too vigorous to breathe: the exuberance of creation which makes the Sibyl of Michelangelo something more than human, which makes Lear something more than human, in one kind or another of divinity.

Balzac's novels are full of strange problems and great passions. He turned aside from nothing which presented itself in nature; and his mind was always turbulent with the magnificent contrasts and caprices of fate. A devouring passion of thought burned on all the situations by which humanity expresses itself, in its flight from the horror of immobility. To say that the situations which he chose are often romantic is but to say that he followed the soul and the senses faithfully on their strangest errands. Our probable novelists of to-day are afraid of whatever emotion might be misinterpreted in a gentleman. Believing, as we do now, in nerves and a fatalistic heredity, we have left but little room for the dignity and disturbance of violent emotion. To Balzac, humanity had not changed since the days when Œdipus was blind and Philoctetes cried in the cave; and equally great miseries were still possible to mortals, though they were French and of the nineteenth century.

And thus he creates, like the poets, a humanity more logical than average life; more typical, more sub-divided among the passions, and having in its veins an energy almost more than human. He realised, as the Greeks did, that human life is made up of elemental passions and necessity; but he was the first to realise that in the modern world the pseudonym of necessity is money. Money and the passions rule the world of his *Human Comedy*.

And, at the root of the passions, determining their action, he saw "those nervous fluids, or that unknown substance which, in default of another term, we must call the will." No word returns oftener to his pen. For him the problem is invariable. Man has a given quantity of energy; each man a different quantity: how will he spend it? A novel is the determination in action of that problem. And he is equally interested in every form of energy, in every egoism, so long as it is fiercely itself. This pre-occupation with the force, rather than with any of its manifestations, gives him his singular impartiality, his absolute lack of prejudice; for it gives him the advantage of an abstract point of view, the unchanging fulcrum for a lever which turns in every direction; and as nothing once set vividly in motion by any form of human activity is without interest for him, he makes every point of his vast chronicle of human affairs equally interesting to his readers.

Baudelaire has observed profoundly that every character in the *Human Comedy* has something of Balzac, has genius. To himself, his own genius was entirely expressed in that word "will." It recurs constantly in his letters. "Men of will are rare!" he cries. And, at a time when he had turned night into day for his labour: "I rise every night with a keener will than that of yesterday." "Nothing wearies me," he says, "neither waiting nor happiness." He exhausts the printers, whose fingers can hardly keep pace with his brain; they call him, he reports proudly, "a man-slayer." And he tries to express himself: "I have always had in me something, I know not what, which made me do differently from others; and, with me, fidelity is perhaps no more than pride. Having only myself to rely upon, I have had to strengthen, to build up that self." There is a scene in *La Cousine Bette* which gives precisely Balzac's own sentiment of the supreme value of energy. The Baron Hulot, ruined on every side, and by his own fault, goes to Josépha, a mistress who had cast him off in the time of his prosperity, and asks her to lodge him for a few days in a garret. She laughs, pities, and then questions him.

" 'Est-ce vrai, vieux,' reprit-elle, 'que tu as tué ton frère et ton oncle, ruiné ta famille, surhypothéqué la maison de tes enfants et mangé la grenouille du gouvernement en Afrique avec la princesse?'

"Le Baron inclina tristement la tête.

" 'Eh bien, j'aime cela!' s'écria Josépha, qui se leva pleine d'enthousiasme. 'C'est un *brûlage* général! c'est sardanapale! c'est grand! c'est complet! On est une canaille, mais on a du cœur.' "

The cry is Balzac's, and it is a characteristic part of his genius to have given it that ironical force by uttering it through the mouth of a Josépha. The joy of the human organism at its highest point of activity: that is what interests him supremely. How passionate, how moving he becomes whenever he has to speak of a real passion, a mania, whether of a lover for his mistress, of a philosopher for his idea, of a miser for his gold, of a Jew dealer for masterpieces! His style clarifies, his words become flesh and blood; he is the lyric poet. And for him every idealism is equal: the gourmandise of Pons is not less serious, nor less sympathetic, not less perfectly realised, than the search of Claës after the Absolute. "The great and terrible clamour of egoism" is the voice to which he is always attentive; "those eloquent faces, proclaiming a soul abandoned to an idea as to a remorse," are the faces with whose history he concerns himself. He drags to light the hidden joys of the *amateur,* and with especial delight those that are hidden deepest, under the most deceptive coverings. He deifies them for their energy, he fashions the world of his *Human Comedy* in their service, as the real world exists, all but passive, to be the pasture of these supreme egoists.

IV

In all that he writes of life, Balzac seeks the soul, but it is the soul as nervous fluid, the executive soul, not the contemplative soul, that, with rare exceptions, he seeks.

He would surprise the motive force of life: that is his *recherche de l'Absolu;* he figures it to himself as almost a substance, and he is the alchemist on its track. "Can man by thinking find out God?" Or life, he would have added; and he would have answered the question with at least a Perhaps.

And of this visionary, this abstract thinker, it must be said that his thought translates itself always into terms of life. Pose before him a purely mental problem, and he will resolve it by a scene in which the problem literally works itself out. It is the quality proper to the novelist, but no novelist ever employed this quality with such persistent activity, and at the same time subordinated action so constantly to the idea. With him action has always a mental basis, is never suffered to intrude for its own sake. He prefers that an episode should seem in itself tedious rather than it should have an illogical interest.

It may be, for he is a Frenchman, that his episodes are sometimes too logical. There are moments when he becomes unreal because he wishes to be too systematic, that is, to be real by measure. He would never have understood the method of Tolstoi, a very stealthy method of surprising life. To Tolstoi life is always the cunning enemy whom one must lull asleep, or noose by an unexpected lasso. He brings in little detail after little detail, seeming to insist on the insignificance of each, in order that it may pass almost unobserved, and be realised only after it has passed. It is his way of disarming the suspiciousness of life.

But Balzac will make no circuit, aims at an open and an unconditional triumph over nature. Thus, when he triumphs, he triumphs signally; and action, in his books, is perpetually crystallising into some phrase, like the single lines of Dante, or some brief scene, in which a whole entanglement comes sharply and suddenly to a luminous point. I will give no instance, for I should have to quote from every volume. I wish rather to remind

myself that there are times when the last fine shade of
a situation seems to have escaped. Even then, the failure
is often more apparent than real, a slight bungling in the
machinery of illusion. Look through the phrase, and you
will find the truth there, perfectly explicit on the other
side of it.

For it cannot be denied, Balzac's style, as style, is
imperfect. It has life, and it has an idea, and it has
variety; there are moments when it attains a rare and
perfectly individual beauty; as when, in *Le Cousin Pons*,
we read of "cette prédisposition aux recherches qui fait
faire à un savant germanique cent lieues dans ses guêtres
pour trouver une vérité qui le regard en riant, assise à
la marge du puits, sous le jasmin de la cour." But I am
far less sure that a student of Balzac would recognise him
in this sentence than that he would recognise the writer
of this other: "Des larmes de pudeur, qui roulèrent entre
les beaux cils de Madame Hulot, arrêtèrent net le garde
national." It is in such passages that the failure in style
is equivalent to a failure in psychology. That his style
should lack symmetry, subordination, the formal virtues
of form, is, in my eyes, a less serious fault. I have often
considered whether, in the novel, perfect form is a good,
or even a possible thing, if the novel is to be what Balzac
made it, history added to poetry. A novelist with style
will not look at life with an entirely naked vision. He
sees through coloured glasses. Human life and human
manners are too various, too moving, to be brought into
the fixity of a quite formal order. There will come a
moment, constantly, when style must suffer, or the closeness and clearness of narration must be sacrificed, some
minute exception of action or psychology must lose its
natural place, or its full emphasis. Balzac, with his rapid
and accumulating mind, without the patience of selection, and without the desire to select where selection
means leaving out something good in itself, if not good in
its place, never hesitates, and his parenthesis comes in.

And often it is into these parentheses that he puts the profoundest part of his thought.

Yet, ready as Balzac is to neglect the story for the philosophy, whenever it seems to him necessary to do so, he would never have admitted that a form of the novel is possible in which the story shall be no more than an excuse for the philosophy. That was because he was a great creator, and not merely a philosophical thinker; because he dealt in flesh and blood, and knew that the passions in action can teach more to the philosopher, and can justify the artist more fully, than all the unacting intellect in the world. He knew that though life without thought was no more than the portion of a dog, yet thoughtful life was more than lifeless thought, and the dramatist more than the commentator. And I cannot help feeling assured that the latest novelists without a story, whatever other merits they certainly have, are lacking in the power to create characters, to express a philosophy in action; and that the form which they have found, however valuable it may be, is the result of this failure, and not either a great refusal or a new vision.

v

The novel as Balzac conceived it has created the modern novel, but no modern novelist has followed, for none has been able to follow, Balzac on his own lines. Even those who have tried to follow him most closely have, sooner or later, branched off in one direction or another, most in the direction indicated by Stendhal. Stendhal has written one book which is a masterpiece, unique in its kind, *Le Rouge et le Noir;* a second, which is full of admirable things, *Le Chartreuse de Parme;* a book of profound criticism, *Racine et Shakespeare;* and a cold and penetrating study of the physiology of love, *De l'Amour,* by the side of which Balzac's *Phy-*

siologie du Mariage is a mere *jeu d'esprit*. He discovered for himself, and for others after him, a method of unemotional, minute, slightly ironical analysis, which has fascinated modern minds, partly because it has seemed to dispense with those difficulties of creation, of creation in the block, which the triumphs of Balzac have only accentuated. Goriot, Valérie Marneffe, Pons, Grandet, Madame de Mortsauf even, are called up before us after the same manner as Othello or Don Quixote; their actions express them so significantly that they seem to be independent of their creator; Balzac stakes all upon each creation, and leaves us no choice but to accept or reject each as a whole, precisely as we should a human being. We do not know all the secrets of their consciousness, any more than we know all the secrets of the consciousness of our friends. But we have only to say "Valérie!" and the woman is before us. Stendhal, on the contrary, undresses Julien's soul in public with a deliberate and fascinating effrontery. There is not a vein of which he does not trace the course, not a wrinkle to which he does not point, not a nerve which he does not touch to the quick. We know everything that passed through his mind, to result probably in some significant inaction. And at the end of the book we know as much about that particular intelligence as the anatomist knows about the body which he has dissected. But meanwhile the life has gone out of the body; and have we, after all, captured a living soul?

I should be the last to say that Julien Sorel is not a creation, but he is not a creation after the order of Balzac; it is a difference of kind; and if we look carefully at Frédéric Moreau, and Madame Gervaisais, and the Abbé Mouret, we shall see that these also, profoundly different as Flaubert and Goncourt and Zola are from Stendhal, are yet more profoundly, more radically, different from the creations of Balzac. Balzac takes a primary passion, puts it into a human body, and sets it to work itself out in visible action. But since Stendhal, novelists have persuaded themselves that the primary passions are a little common, or noisy, or a little heavy to handle, and they have concerned themselves with passions tempered by reflection, and the sensations of elaborate brains. It was Stendhal who substituted the brain for the heart, as the battle-place of the novel; not the brain as Balzac conceived it, a motive-force of action, the mainspring of passion, the force by which a nature directs its accumulated energy; but a sterile sort of brain, set at a great distance from the heart, whose rhythm is too faint to disturb it. We have been intellectualising upon Stendhal ever since, until the persons of the modern novel have come to resemble those diaphanous jelly-fish, with balloon-like heads and the merest tufts of bodies, which float up and down in the Aquarium at Naples.

Thus, coming closer, as it seems, to what is called reality, in this banishment of great emotions, and this attention upon the sensations, modern analytic novelists are really getting further and further from that life which is the one certain thing in the world. Balzac employs all his detail to call up a tangible world about his men and women, not, perhaps, understanding the full power of detail as psychology, as Flaubert is to understand it; but, after all, his detail is only the background of the picture; and there, stepping out of the canvas, as the sombre people of Velazquez step out of their canvases at the Prado, is the living figure, looking into your eyes with eyes that respond to you like a mirror.

The novels of Balzac are full of electric fluid. To take up one of them is to feel the shock of life, as one feels it on touching certain magnetic hands. To turn over volume after volume is like wandering through the streets of a great city, at that hour of the night when human activity is at its full. There is a particular kind of excitement inherent in the very aspect of a modern city, of London or Paris; in the mere sensation of being in its midst, in the sight of all those active and fatigued faces which pass so rapidly; of those long and endless streets, full of houses, each of which is like the body of a multiform soul, looking out through the eyes of many windows. There is something intoxicating in the lights, the movement of shadows under the lights, the vast and billowy sound of that shadowy movement. And there is something more than this mere unconscious action upon the nerves. Every step in a great city is a step into an unknown world. A new future is possible at every street corner. I never know, when I go out into one of those crowded streets, but that the whole course of my life may be changed before I return to the house I have quitted.

I am writing these lines in Madrid, to which I have come suddenly, after a long quiet in Andalusia; and I feel already a new pulse in my blood, a keener consciousness of life, and a sharper human curiosity. Even in Seville I knew that I should see to-morrow, in the same streets, hardly changed since the Middle Ages, the same people that I had seen to-day. But here there are new possibilities, all the exciting accidents of the modern world, of a population always changing, of a city into which civilisation has brought all its unrest. And as I walk in these broad, windy streets and see these people, whom I hardly recognise for Spaniards, so awake and so hybrid are they, I have felt the sense of Balzac coming back into my veins. At Cordova he was unthinkable; at Cadiz I could realise only his large, universal outlines, vague as the murmur of the sea; here I feel him, he speaks the language I am talking, he sums up the life in whose midst I find myself.

For Balzac is the equivalent of great cities. He is bad reading for solitude, for he fills the mind with the nostalgia of cities. When a man speaks to me familiarly of Balzac I know already something of the man with whom I have to do. "The physiognomy of women does not begin before the age of thirty," he has said; and perhaps before that age no one can really understand Balzac. Few young people care for him, for there is

nothing in him that appeals to the senses except through
the intellect. Not many women care for him supremely,
for it is part of his method to express sentiments through
facts, and not facts through sentiments. But it is natural
that he should be the favourite reading of men of the
world, of those men of the world who have the distinction
of their kind; for he supplies the key of the enigma which
they are studying.

VI

The life of Balzac was one long labour, in which time,
money, and circumstances were all against him. In 1835
he writes: "I have lately spent twenty-six days in my study
without leaving it. I took the air only at that window
which dominates Paris, which I mean to dominate." And
he exults in the labour: "If there is any glory in that,
I alone could accomplish such a feat." He symbolises the
course of his life in comparing it to the sea beating
against a rock: "To-day one flood, to-morrow another,
bears me along with it. I am dashed against a rock,
I recover myself and go on to another reef. . . . Sometimes it seems to me that my brain is on fire. I shall die
in the trenches of the intellect."

Balzac, like Scott, died under the weight of his debts;
and it would seem, if one took him at his word, that the
whole of the *Human Comedy* was written for money. In
the modern world, as he himself realised more clearly
than any one, money is more often a symbol than an
entity, and it can be the symbol of every desire. For
Balzac money was the key of his earthly paradise. It
meant leisure to visit the woman whom he loved, and at
the end it meant the possibility of marrying her.

There were only two women in Balzac's life: one, a
woman much older than himself, of whom he wrote, on
her death, to the other: "She was a mother, a friend, a
family, a companion, a counsel, she made the writer, she
consoled the young man, she formed his taste, she wept

like a sister, she laughed, she came every day, like a healing slumber, to put sorrow to sleep." The other was Mme. de Hanska, whom he married in 1850, three months before his death. He had loved her for twenty years; she was married, and lived in Poland; it was only at rare intervals that he was able to see her, and then very briefly; but his letters to her, published since his death, are a simple, perfectly individual, daily record of a great passion. For twenty years he existed on a divine certainty without a future, and almost without a present. But we see the force of that sentiment passing into his work; *Séraphita* is its ecstasy, everywhere is its human shadow; it refines his strength, it gives him surprising intuitions, it gives him all that was wanting to his genius. Mme. de Hanska is the heroine of the *Human Comedy*, as Beatrice is the heroine of the *Divine Comedy*.

A great lover, to whom love, as well as every other passion and the whole visible world, was an idea, a flaming spiritual perception, Balzac enjoyed the vast happiness of the idealist. Contentedly, joyously, he sacrificed every petty enjoyment to the idea of love, the idea of fame, and to that need of the organism to exercise its forces, which is the only definition of genius. I do not know, among the lives of men of letters, a life better filled, or more appropriate. A young man who, for a short time, was his secretary, declared: "I would not live your life for the fame of Napoleon and of Byron combined!" The Comte de Gramont did not realise, as the world in general does not realise, that, to the man of creative energy, creation is at once a necessity and a joy, and to the lover, hope in absence is the elixir of life. Balzac tasted more than all earthly pleasures as he sat there in his attic, creating the world over again, that he might lay it at the feet of a woman. Certainly to him there was no tedium in life, for there was no hour without its vivid employment, and no moment in which to perceive the most desolate of all certainties, that hope is in the past. His death was as fortunate as his life; he died at the

height of his powers, at the height of his fame, at the
moment of the fulfilment of his happiness, and perhaps
of the too sudden relief of that delicate burden.

PROSPER MÉRIMÉE

I

STENDHAL has left us a picture of Mérimée as "a young
man in a grey frock-coat, very ugly, and with a turned-up
nose. . . . This young man had something insolent and
extremely unpleasant about him. His eyes, small and
without expression, had always the same look, and this
look was ill-natured. . . . Such was my first impression
of the best of my present friends. I am not too sure of
his heart, but I am sure of his talents. It is M. le Comte
Gazul, now so well known; a letter from him, which came
to me last week, made me happy for two days. His
mother has a good deal of French wit and a superior intelligence. Like her son, it seems to me that she might
give way to emotion once a year." There, painted by a
clear-sighted and disinterested friend, is a picture of
Mérimée almost from his own point of view, or at least
as he would himself have painted the picture. How far
is it, in its insistence on the *attendrissement une fois par
an,* on the subordination of natural feelings to a somewhat disdainful aloofness, the real Mérimée?

Early in life, Mérimée adopted his theory, fixed his
attitude, and to the end of his life he seemed, to those
about him, to have walked along the path he had chosen,
almost without a deviation. He went to England at the
age of twenty-three, to Spain four years later, and might
seem to have been drawn naturally to those two countries,
to which he was to return so often, by natural affinities
of temper and manner. It was the English manner that
he liked, that came naturally to him; the correct, unmoved exterior, which is a kind of positive strength, not

to be broken by any onslaught of events or emotions; and in Spain he found an equally positive animal acceptance of things as they are, which satisfied his profound, restrained, really Pagan sensuality, Pagan in the hard, eighteenth-century sense. From the beginning he was a student, of art, of history, of human nature, and we find him enjoying, in his deliberate, keen way, the studied diversions of the student; body and soul each kept exactly in its place, each provided for without partiality. He entered upon literature by a mystification, *Le Théâtre de Clara Gazul,* a book of plays supposed to be translated from a living Spanish dramatist; and he followed it by *La Guzla,* another mystification, a book of prose ballads supposed to be translated from the Illyrian. And these mystifications, like the forgeries of Chatterton, contain perhaps the most sincere, the most undisguised emotion which he ever permitted himself to express; so secure did he feel of the heart behind the pearl necklace of the *décolletée* Spanish actress, who travesties his own face in the frontispiece to the one, and so remote from himself did he feel the bearded gentleman to be, who sits cross-legged on the ground, holding his lyre or *guzla,* in the frontispiece to the other. Then came a historical novel, the *Chronique du Règne de Charles IX,* before he discovered, as if by accident, precisely what it was he was meant to do: the short story. Then he drifted into history, became Inspector of Ancient Monuments, and helped to save Vézelay, among other good deeds towards art, done in his cold, systematic, after all satisfactory manner. He travelled at almost regular intervals, not only in Spain and England, but in Corsica, in Greece and Asia Minor, in Italy, in Hungary, in Bohemia, usually with a definite, scholarly object, and always with an alert attention to everything that came in his way, to the manners of people, their national characters, their differences from one another. An intimate friend of the Countess de Montijo, the mother of the Empress Eugénie, he was a friend, not a courtier, at the court of the Third

Empire. He was elected to the Academy, mainly for his
Études sur l'Histoire Romaine, a piece of dry history, and
immediately scandalised his supporters by publishing a
story, *Arsène Guillot,* which was taken for a veiled attack
on religion and on morals. Soon after, his imagination
seemed to flag; he abandoned himself, perhaps a little
wearily, more and more to facts, to the facts of history
and learning; learned Russian, and translated Pushkin
and Turgenev; and died in 1870, at Cannes, perhaps
less satisfied with himself than most men who have done,
in their lives, far less exactly what they have intended to
do.

"I have theories about the very smallest things—gloves,
boots, and the like," says Mérimée in one of his letters;
des idées très-arrêtées, as he adds with emphasis in
another. Precise opinions lead easily to prejudices, and
Mérimée, who prided himself on the really very logical
quality of his mind, put himself somewhat deliberately
into the hands of his prejudices. Thus he hated religion,
distrusted priests, would not let himself be carried away
by any instinct of admiration, would not let himself do
the things which he had the power to do, because his
other, critical self came mockingly behind him, suggesting
that very few things were altogether worth doing. "There
is nothing that I despise and even detest so much as
humanity in general," he confesses in a letter; and it is
with a certain self-complacency that he defines the only
kind of society in which he found himself at home: "(1)
With unpretentious people whom I have known a long
time; (2) in a Spanish *venta,* with muleteers and peasant
women of Andalusia." One day, as he finds himself in a
pensive mood, dreaming of a woman, he translates for her
some lines of Sophocles, into verse, "English verse, you
understand, for I abhor French verse." The carefulness
with which he avoids received opinions shows a certain
consciousness of those opinions, which in a more imag-
inatively independent mind would scarcely have found
a place. It is not only for an effect, but more and more

genuinely, that he sets his acquirements as a scholar above his accomplishments as an artist. Clearing away, as it seemed to him, every illusion from before his eyes, he forgot the last illusion of positive people: the possibility that one's eyes may be short-sighted.

Mérimée realises a type which we are accustomed to associate almost exclusively with the eighteenth century, but of which our own time can offer us many obscure examples. It is the type of the *esprit fort:* the learned man, the choice, narrow artist, who is at the same time the cultivated sensualist. To such a man the pursuit of women is part of his constant pursuit of human experience, and of the document, which is the summing up of human experience. To Mérimée history itself was a matter of detail. "In history, I care only for anecdotes," he says in the preface to the *Chronique du Règne de Charles IX*. And he adds: "It is not a very noble taste; but I confess to my shame, I would willingly give Thucydides for the authentic memoirs of Aspasia or of a slave of Pericles; for only memoirs, which are the familiar talk of an author with his reader, afford those portraits of *man* which amuse and interest me." This curiosity of mankind above all things, and of mankind at home, or in private actions, not necessarily of any import to the general course of the world, leads the curious searcher naturally to the more privately interesting and the less publicly important half of mankind. Not scrupulous in arriving at any end by the most adaptable means, not disturbed by any illusions as to the physical facts of the universe, a sincere and grateful lover of variety, doubtless an amusing companion with those who amused him, Mérimée found much of his entertainments and instruction, at all events in his younger years, in that "half world" which he tells us he frequented "very much out of curiosity, living in it always as in a foreign country." Here, as elsewhere, Mérimée played the part of the amateur. He liked anecdotes, not great events, in his history; and he was careful to avoid any too serious pas-

sions in his search for sensations. There, no doubt, for
the sensualist, is happiness, if he can resign himself to it.
It is only serious passions which make anybody unhappy;
and Mérimée was carefully on the lookout against a possible unhappiness. I can imagine him ending every day
with satisfaction, and beginning every fresh day with just
enough expectancy to be agreeable, at that period of
his life when he was writing the finest of his stories, and
dividing the rest of his leisure between the drawing-rooms
and the pursuit of uneventful adventures.

Only, though we are *automates autant qu'esprit,* as
Pascal tells us, it is useless to expect that what is
automatic in us should remain invariable and uncon-
ditioned. If life could be lived on a plan, and for such
men on such a plan, if first impulses and profound passions could be kept entirely out of one's own experience,
and studied only at a safe distance, then, no doubt, one
could go on being happy, in a not too heroic way. But,
with Mérimée as with all the rest of the world, the
scheme breaks down one day, just when a reasonable
solution to things seems to have been arrived at. Mérimée
had already entered on a peaceable enough *liaison* when
the first letter came to him from the *Inconnue* to whom
he was to write so many letters, for nine years without
seeing her, and then for thirty years more after he had
met her, the last letter being written but two hours before
his death. These letters, which we can now read in two
volumes, have a delicately insincere sincerity which makes
every letter a work of art, not because he tried to make
it so, but because he could not help seeing the form
simultaneously with the feeling, and writing genuine love-
letters with an excellence almost as impersonal as that of
his stories. He begins with curiosity, which passes with
singular rapidity into a kind of self-willed passion; already in the eighth letter, long before he has seen her, he
is speculating which of the two will know best how to
torture the other: that is, as he views it, love best. "We
shall never love one another really," he tells her, as he

begins to hope for the contrary. Then he discovers, for the first time, and without practical result, "that it is better to have illusions than to have none at all." He confesses himself to her, sometimes reminding her: "You will never know either all the good or all the evil that I have in me. I have spent my life in being praised for qualities which I do not possess, and calumniated for defects which are not mine." And, with a strange, weary humility, which is the other side of his contempt for most things and people, he admits: "To you I am like an old opera, which you are obliged to forget, in order to see it again with any pleasure." He, who has always distrusted first impulses, finds himself telling her (was she really so like him, or was he arguing with himself?) : "You always fear first impulses; do not you see that they are the only ones which are worth anything and which always succeed?" Does he realise, unable to change the temperament which he has partly made for himself, that just there has been his own failure?

Perhaps of all love-letters, these of Mérimée show us love triumphing over the most carefully guarded personality. Here the obstacle is not duty, nor circumstance, nor a rival; but (on her side as on his, it would seem) a carefully trained natural coldness, in which action, and even for the most part feeling, are relinquished to the control of second thoughts. A habit of repressive irony goes deep: Mérimée might well have thought himself secure against the outbreak of an unconditional passion. Yet here we find passion betraying itself, often only by bitterness, together with a shy, surprising tenderness, in this curious lovers' itinerary, marked out with all the customary sign-posts, and leading, for all its wilful deviations, along the inevitable road.

It is commonly supposed that the artist, by the habit of his profession, has made for himself a sort of cuirass of phrases against the direct attack of emotion, and so will suffer less than most people if he should fall into love, and things should not go altogether well with him.

Rather, he is the more laid open to attack, the more helplessly entangled when once the net has been cast over him. He lives through every passionate trouble, not merely with the daily emotions of the crowd, but with the whole of his imagination. Pain is multiplied to him by the force of that faculty by which he conceives delight. What is most torturing in every not quite fortunate love is memory, and the artist becomes an artist by his intensification of memory. Mérimée has himself defined art as exaggeration *à propos*. Well, to the artist his own life is an exaggeration not *à propos,* and every hour dramatises for him its own pain and pleasure, in a tragic comedy of which he is the author and actor and spectator. The practice of art is a sharpening of the sensations, and, the knife once sharpened, does it cut into one's hand less deeply because one is in the act of using it to carve wood?

And so we find Mérimée, the most impersonal of artists, and one of those most critical of the caprices and violences of fate, giving in to an almost obvious temptation, an anonymous correspondence, a mysterious unknown woman, and passing from stage to stage of a finally very genuine love-affair, which kept him in a fluttering agitation for more than thirty years. It is curious to note that the little which we know of this *Inconnue* seems to mark her out as the realisation of a type which had always been Mérimée's type of woman. She has the "wicked eyes" of all his heroines, from the Mariquita of his first attempt in literature, who haunts the Inquisitor with "her great black eyes, like the eyes of a young cat, soft and wicked at once." He finds her at the end of his life, in a novel of Turgenev, "one of those diabolical creatures whose coquetry is the more dangerous because it is capable of passion." Like so many artists, he has invented his ideal before he meets it, and must have seemed almost to have fallen in love with his own creation. It is one of the privileges of art to create nature, as, according to a certain mystical doctrine, you can actualise, by sheer fixity of contemplation, your mental image of a thing into the thing itself. The *Inconnue* was one of a series, the rest imaginary; and her power over Mérimée, we can hardly doubt, came not only from her queer likeness of temperament to his, but from the singular, flattering pleasure which it must have given him to find that he had invented with so much truth to nature.

II

Mérimée as a writer belongs to the race of Laclos and of Stendhal, a race essentially French; and we find him representing, a little coldly, as it seemed, the claims of mere unimpassioned intellect, at work on passionate problems, among those people of the Romantic period to whom emotion, evident emotion, was everything. In his subjects he is as "Romantic" as Victor Hugo or Gautier; he adds, even, a peculiar flavour of cruelty to the Romantic ingredients. But he distinguishes sharply, as French writers before him had so well known how to do, between the passion one is recounting and the moved or unmoved way in which one chooses to tell it. To Mérimée art was a very formal thing, almost a part of learning; it was a thing to be done with a clear head, reflectively, with a calm mastery of even the most vivid material. While others, at that time, were intoxicating themselves with strange sensations, hoping that "nature would take the pen out of their hands and write," just at the moment when their own thoughts became least coherent, Mérimée went quietly to work over something a little abnormal which he had found in nature, with as disinterested, as scholarly, as mentally reserved an interest as if it were one of those Gothic monuments which he inspected to such good purpose, and, as it has seemed to his biographer, with so little sympathy. His own emotion, so far as it is roused, seems to him an extraneous thing, a thing to be concealed, if not a little ashamed of. It is the thing itself he wishes to give you, not his feelings about it; and his theory is that if the thing itself can only be made to stand and speak before the reader, the reader will supply for himself all the feeling that is needed, all the feeling that would be called out in nature by a perfectly clear sight of just such passions in action. It seems to him bad art to paint the picture, and to write a description of the picture as well.

And his method serves him wonderfully up to a certain point, and then leaves him, without his being well aware of it, at the moment even when he has convinced himself that he has realised the utmost of his aim. At a time when he had come to consider scholarly dexterity as the most important part of art, Mérimée tells us that *La Vénus d'Ille* seemed to him the best story he had ever written. He has often been taken at his word, but to take him at his word is to do him an injustice. *La Vénus d'Ille* is a modern setting of the old story of the Ring given to Venus, and Mérimée has been praised for the ingenuity with which he has obtained an effect of supernatural terror, while leaving the way open for a material explanation of the supernatural. What he has really done is to materialise a myth, by accepting in it precisely what might be a mere superstition, the form of the thing, and leaving out the spiritual meaning of which that form was no more than a temporary expression. The ring which the bridegroom sets on the finger of Venus, and which the statue's finger closes upon, accepting it, symbolises the pact between love and sensuality, the lover's abdication of all but the physical part of love; and the statue taking its place between husband and wife on the marriage-night, and crushing life out of him in an inexorable embrace, symbolises the merely natural destruction which that granted prayer brings with it, as a merely human Messalina takes her lover on his own terms, in his abandonment of all to Venus. Mérimée sees a cruel and fantastic superstition, which he is afraid of seeming to take too seriously, which he prefers to leave as a story of ghosts or bogies, a thing at which we are to shiver as at a mere twitch on the nerves, while our mental confidence in the impossibility of what we cannot explain is preserved for us by a hint at a muleteer's vengeance. "Have I frightened you?" says the man of the world, with a reassuring smile. "Think about it no more; I really meant nothing."

And yet, does he after all mean nothing? The devil, the old pagan gods, the spirits of evil incarnated under every form, fascinated him; it gave him a malign pleasure to set them at their evil work among men, while, all the time, he mocks them and the men who believed in them. He is a materialist, and yet he believes in at least a something evil, outside the world, or in the heart of it, which sets humanity at its strange games, relentlessly. Even then he will not surrender his doubts, his ironies, his negations. Is he, perhaps, at times, the athiest who fears that, after all, God may exist, or at least who realises how much he would fear him if he did exist?

Mérimée had always delighted in mystifications; he was always on his guard against being mystified himself, either by nature or by his fellow-creatures. In the early "Romantic" days he had had a genuine passion for various things: "local colour," for instance. But even then he had invented it by a kind of trick, and, later on, he explains what a poor thing "local colour" is, since it can so easily be invented without leaving one's study. He is full of curiosity, and will go far to satisfy it, regretting "the decadence," in our times, "of energetic passions, in favour of tranquillity and perhaps of happiness." These energetic passions he will find, indeed, in our own times, in Corsica, in Spain, in Lithuania, really in the midst of a very genuine and profoundly studied "local colour," and also, under many disguises, in Parisian drawing-rooms. Mérimée prized happiness, material comfort, the satisfaction of one's immediate desires, very highly, and it was his keen sense of life, of the pleasures of living, that gave him some of his keenness in the realisation of violent death, physical pain, whatever disturbs the equilibrium of things with unusual emphasis. Himself really selfish, he can distinguish the unhappiness of others with a kind of intuition which is not sympathy, but which selfish people often have: a dramatic consciousness of how painful pain must be, whoever feels it. It is not pity, though it communicates itself to us, often enough, as pity. It is the clear-sighted sensitiveness of a man who watches human things closely, bringing them home to himself with the deliberate, essaying art of an actor who has to represent a particular passion in movement.

And always in Mérimée there is this union of curiosity with indifference: the curiosity of the student, the indifference of the man of the world. Indifference, in him, as in the man of the world, is partly an attitude, adopted for its form, and influencing the temperament just so much as gesture always influences emotion. The man who forces himself to appear calm under excitement teaches his nerves to follow instinctively the way he has shown them. In time he will not merely seem calm but will be calm, at the moment when he learns that a great disaster has befallen him. But, in Mérimée, was the indifference even as external as it must always be when there is restraint, when, therefore, there is something to restrain? Was there not in him a certain drying up of the sources of emotion, as the man of the world came to accept almost the point of view of society, reading his stories to a little circle of court ladies, when, once in a while, he permitted himself to write a story? And was not this increase of well-bred indifference, now more than ever characteristic, almost the man himself, the chief reason why he abandoned art so early, writing only two or three short stories during the last twenty-five years of his life, and writing these with a labour which by no means conceals itself?

Mérimée had an abstract interest in, almost an enthusiasm for, facts; facts for their meaning, the light they throw on psychology. He declines to consider psychology except through its expression in facts, with an impersonality far more real than that of Flaubert. The document, historical or social, must translate itself into sharp action before he can use it; not that he does not see, and appreciate better than most others, all there is of significance in the document itself; but his theory or art is inexorable. He never allowed himself to write as he pleased, but he wrote always as he considered the artist should write. Thus he made for himself a kind of formula, confining himself, as some thought, within too narrow limits, but, to himself, doing exactly what he set himself to do, with all the satisfaction of one who is convinced of the justice of his aim and confident of his power to attain it.

Look, for instance, at his longest, far from his best work, *La Chronique du Règne de Charles IX*. Like so much of his work, it has something of the air of a *tour de force,* not taken up entirely for its own sake. Mérimée drops into a fashion, half deprecatingly, as if he sees through it, and yet, as with merely mundane elegance, with a resolve to be more scrupulously exact than its devotees. "Belief," says some one in this book, as if speaking for Mérimée, "is a precious gift which has been denied me." Well, he will do better, without belief, than those who believe. Written under a title which suggests a work of actual history, it is more than possible that the first suggestion of this book really came, as he tells us in the preface, from the reading of "a large number of memoirs and pamphlets relating to the end of the sixteenth century. . . . I wished to make an epitome of my reading," he tells us, "and here is the epitome." The historical problem attracted him, that never quite explicable Massacre of St. Bartholomew, in which there was precisely the violence of action and uncertainty of motive which he liked to set before him at the beginning of a task in literature. Probable, clearly defined people, in the dress of the period, grew up naturally about this central motive; humour and irony have their part; there are adventures, told with a sword's point of sharpness, and in the fewest possible words; there is one of his cruel and loving women, in whom every sentiment becomes action, by some twisted feminine logic of their own. It is the most artistic, the most clean-cut, of historical novels; and yet this perfect neatness of method suggests a certain indifference on the part of the writer, as if he were more interested in doing the thing well than in doing it.

And that, in all but the very best of his stories (even, perhaps, in *Arsène Guillot* only not in such perfect things as *Carmen,* as *Mateo Falcone*), is what Mérimée just lets us see, underneath an almost faultless skill of narrative. An incident told by Mérimée at his best gathers about it something of the gravity of history, the composed way in which it is told helping to give it the equivalent of remoteness, allowing it not merely to be, but, what is more difficult, to seem classic in its own time. "Magnificent things, things after my own heart—that is to say, Greek in their truth and simplicity," he writes in a letter, referring to the tales of Pushkin. The phrase is scarcely too strong to apply to what is best in his own work. Made out of elemental passions, hard, cruel, detached as it were from their own sentiments, the stories that he tells might in other hands become melodramas: *Carmen,* taken thoughtlessly out of his hands, has supplied the libretto to the most popular of modern light operas. And yet, in his severe method of telling, mere outlines, it seems, told with an even stricter watch over what is significantly left out than over what is briefly allowed to be said in words, these stories sum up little separate pieces of the world, each a little world in itself. And each is a little world which he has made his own, with a labor at last its own reward, and taking life partly because he has put into it more of himself than the mere intention of doing it well. Mérimée loved Spain, and *Carmen,* which, by some caprice of popularity, is the symbol of Spain to people in general, is really, to those

who know Spain well, the most Spanish thing that has
been written since *Gil Blas*. All the little parade of local
colour and philology, the appendix on the *Calo* of the
gypsies, done to heighten the illusion, has more significance than people sometimes think. In this story all
the qualities of Mérimée come into agreement; the student of human passions, the traveller, the observer, the
learned man, meet in harmony; and, in addition, there
is the *aficionado*, the true *amateur*, in love with Spain
and the Spaniards.

It is significant that at the reception of Mérimée at the
Académie Française in 1845, M. Étienne thought it already needful to say: "Do not pause in the midst of your
career; rest is not permitted to your talent." Already
Mérimée was giving way to facts, to facts in themselves,
as they come into history, into records of scholarship.
We find him writing, a little dryly, on Catiline, on
Cæsar, on Don Pedro the Cruel, learning Russian, and
translating from it (yet, while studying the Russians
before all the world, never discovering the mystical Russian soul), writing learned articles, writing reports. He
looked around on contemporary literature, and found
nothing that he could care for. Stendhal was gone, and
who else was there to admire? Flaubert, it seemed to
him, was "wasting his talent under the pretence of
realism." Victor Hugo was "a fellow with the most
beautiful figures of speech at his disposal," who did not
take the trouble to think, but intoxicated himself with
his own words. Baudelaire made him furious, Renan
filled him with pitying scorn. In the midst of his contempt, he may perhaps have imagined that he was being
left behind. For whatever reason, weakness or strength,
he could not persuade himself that it was worth while to
strive for anything any more. He died probably at the
moment when he was no longer a fashion, and had not
yet become a classic.

THÉOPHILE GAUTIER

I

GAUTIER has spoken for himself in a famous passage of *Mademoiselle de Maupin*: "I am a man of the Homeric age; the world in which I live is not my world, and I understand nothing of the society which surrounds me. For me Christ did not come; I am as much a pagan as Alcibiades or Phidias. I have never plucked on Golgotha the flowers of the Passion, and the deep stream that flows from the side of the Crucified and sets a crimson girdle about the world, has never washed me in its flood; my rebellious body will not acknowledge the supremacy of the soul, and my flesh will not endure to be mortified. I find the earth as beautiful as the sky, and I think that perfection of form is virtue. I have no gift for spirituality; I prefer a statue to a ghost, full noon to twilight. Three things delight me: gold, marble, and purple; brilliance, solidity, colour. . . . I have looked on love in the light of antiquity, and as a piece of sculpture more or less perfect. . . . All my life I have been concerned with the form of the flagon, never with the quality of its contents." That is part of a confession of faith, and it is spoken with absolute sincerity. Gautier knew himself, and could tell the truth about himself as simply, as impartially, as if he had been describing a work of art. Or is he not, indeed, describing a work of art? Was not that very state of mind, that finished and limited temperament, a thing which he had collaborated with nature in making, with an effective heightening of what was most natural to him, in the spirit of art?

Gautier saw the world as mineral, as metal, as pigment, as rock, tree, water, as architecture, costume, under sunlight, gas, in all the colours that light can bring out of built or growing things; he saw it as contour, movement; he saw all that a painter sees, when the painter

sets himself to copy, not to create. He was the finest
copyist who ever used paint with a pen. Nothing that
can be expressed in technical terms escaped him; there
were no technical terms which he could not reduce to
an orderly beauty. But he absorbed all this visible world
with the hardly discriminating impartiality of the retina;
he had no moods, was not to be distracted by a sentiment,
heard no voices, saw nothing but darkness, the negation
of day, in night. He was tirelessly attentive, he had no
secrets of his own and could keep none of nature's. He
could describe every ray of the nine thousand precious
stones in the throne of Ivan the Terrible, in the Treasury
of the Kremlin; but he could tell you nothing of one of
Maeterlinck's bees.

The five senses made Gautier for themselves, that they
might become articulate. He speaks for them all with a
dreadful unconcern. All his words are in love with
matter, and they enjoy their lust and have no recollection. If the body did not dwindle and expand to some
ignoble physical conclusion; if wrinkles did not creep
yellowing up women's necks, and the fire in a man's blood
did not lose its heat; he would always be content. Everything that he cared for in the world was to be had, except,
perhaps, rest from striving after it; only, everything would
one day come to an end, after a slow spoiling. Decrepit,
colourless, uneager things shocked him, and it was with
an acute, almost disinterested pity that he watched himself die.

All his life Gautier adored life, and all the processes
and forms of life. A pagan, a young Roman, hard and
delicate, with something of cruelty in his sympathy with
things that could be seen and handled, he would have
hated the soul, if he had ever really apprehended it, for
its qualifying and disturbing power upon the body. No
other modern writer, no writer perhaps, has described
nakedness with so abstract a heat of rapture: like d'Albert
when he sees Mlle. de Maupin for the first and last time,
he is the artist before he is the lover, and he is the lover

while he is the artist. It was above all things the human body whose contours and colours he wished to fix for eternity, in the "robust art" of "verse, marble, onyx, enamel." And it was not the body as a frail, perishable thing, and a thing to be pitied, that he wanted to perpetuate; it was the beauty of life itself, imperishable at least in its recurrence.

He loved imperishable things: the body, as generation after generation refashions it, the world, as it is restored and rebuilt, and then gems, and hewn stone, and carved ivory, and woven tapestry. He loved verse for its solid, strictly limited, resistant form, which, while prose melts and drifts about it, remains unalterable, indestructible. Words, he knew, can build as strongly as stones, and not merely rise to music, like the walls of Troy, but be themselves music as well as structure. Yet, as in visible things he cared only for hard outline and rich colour, so in words too he had no love of half-tints, and was content to do without that softening of atmosphere which was to be prized by those who came after him as the thing most worth seeking. Even his verse is without mystery; if he meditates, his meditation has all the fixity of a kind of sharp, precise criticism.

What Gautier saw he saw with unparalleled exactitude; he allows himself no poetic license or room for fine phrases; has his eye always on the object, and really uses the words which best describe it, whatever they may be. So his books of travel are guide-books, in addition to being other things; and not by any means "states of soul" or states of nerves. He is willing to give you information, and able to give it to you without deranging his periods. The little essay on Leonardo is an admirable piece of artistic divination, and it is also a clear, simple, sufficient account of the man, his temperament, and his way of work. The study of Baudelaire, reprinted in the *édition définitive* of the *Fleurs du Mal,* remains the one satisfactory summing up, it is not a solution, of the enigma which Baudelaire personified; and it is almost

the most coloured and perfumed thing in words which
he ever wrote. He wrote equally well about cities, poets,
novelists, painters, or sculptors; he did not understand
one better than the other, or feel less sympathy for one
than for another. He, the "parfait magicien des lettres
françaises," to whom faultless words came in faultlessly
beautiful order, could realise, against Balzac himself, that
Balzac had a style: "he possesses, though he did not
think so, a style, and a very beautiful style, the necessary,
inevitable, mathematical style of his ideas." He appreciated Ingres as justly as he appreciated El Greco; he
went through the Louvre, room by room, saying the right
thing about each painter in turn. He did not say the
final thing; he said nothing which we have to pause
and think over before we see the whole of its truth or
apprehend the whole of its beauty. Truth, in him, comes
to us almost literally through the eyesight, and with the
same beautiful clearness as if it were one of those visible
things which delighted him most: gold, marble, and
purple; brilliance, solidity, colour.

GUSTAVE FLAUBERT

Salammbô is an attempt, as Flaubert, himself his best
critic, has told us, to "perpetuate a mirage by applying
to antiquity the methods of the modern novel." By the
modern novel he means the novel as he had reconstructed
it; he means Madame Bovary. That perfect book is perfect because Flaubert had, for once, found exactly the subject suited to his method, had made his method and his
subject one. On his scientific side Flaubert is a realist,
but there is another, perhaps a more intimately personal
side, on which he is lyrical, lyrical in a large, sweeping
way. The lyric poet in him made La Tentation de Saint-
Antoine, the analyst made L'Éducation Sentimentale;
but in Madame Bovary we find the analyst and the lyric
poet in equilibrium. It is the history of a woman, as

carefully observed as any story that has ever been written, and observed in surroundings of the most ordinary kind. But Flaubert finds the romantic material which he loved, the materials of beauty, in precisely that temperament which he studies so patiently and so cruelly. Madame Bovary is a little woman, half vulgar and half hysterical, incapable of a fine passion; but her trivial desires, her futile aspirations after second-rate pleasures and second-hand ideals, give to Flaubert all that he wants: the opportunity to create beauty out of reality. What is common in the imagination of Madame Bovary becomes exquisite in Flaubert's rendering of it, and by that counterpoise of a commonness in the subject he is saved from any vague ascents of rhetoric in his rendering of it.

In writing *Salammbô* Flaubert set himself to renew the historical novel, as he had renewed the novel of manners. He would have admitted, doubtless, that perfect success in the historical novel is impossible, by the nature of the case. We are at best only half conscious of the reality of the things about us, only able to translate them approximately into any form of art. How much is left over, in the closest transcription of a mere line of houses in a street, of a passing steamer, of one's next-door neighbour, of the point of view of a foreigner looking along Piccadilly, of one's own state of mind, moment by moment, as one walks from Oxford Circus to the Marble Arch? Think, then, of the attempts to reconstruct no matter what period of the past, to distinguish the difference in the aspect of a world perhaps bossed with castles and ridged with ramparts, to two individualities encased within chain-armour! Flaubert chose his antiquity wisely: a period of which we know too little to confuse us, a city of which no stone is left on another, the minds of Barbarians who have left us no psychological documents. "Be sure I have made no fantastic Carthage," he says proudly, pointing to his documents: Ammianus Marcellinus, who has furnished him with "the *exact* form of a door"; the Bible and Theophrastus, from which he obtains his perfumes and his precious stones; Gesenius, from whom he gets his Punic names; the *Mémoires de l'Académie des Inscriptions*. "As for the temple of Tanit, I am sure of having reconstructed it as it was, with the treatise of the Syrian Goddess, with the medals of the Duc de Luynes, with what is known of the temple at Jerusalem, with a passage of St. Jerome, quoted by Seldon (*De Diis Syriis*), with the plan of the temple of Gozzo, which is quite Carthaginian, and best of all, with the ruins of the temple of Thugga, which I have seen myself, with my own eyes, and of which no traveller or anti-quarian, so far as I know, has ever spoken." But that, after all, as he admits (when, that is, he has proved point by point his minute accuracy to all that is known of ancient Carthage, his faithfulness to every indication which can serve for his guidance, his patience in grouping rather than his daring in the invention of action and details), that is not the question. "I care little enough for archæology! If the colour is not uniform, if the details are out of keeping, if the manners do not spring from the religion and the actions from the passions, if the characters are not consistent, if the costumes are not appropriate to the habits and the architecture to the climate, if, in a word, there is not harmony, I am in error. If not, no."

And there, precisely, is the definition of the one merit which can give a historical novel the right to exist, and at the same time a definition of the merit which sets *Salammbô* above all other historical novels. Everything in the book is strange, some of it might easily be bewilder-ing, some revolting; but all is in harmony. The harmony is like that of Eastern music, not immediately conveying its charm, or even the secret of its measure, to Western ears; but a monotony coiling perpetually upon itself, after a severe law of its own. Or rather, it is like a fresco, painted gravely in hard, definite colours, firmly detached from a background of burning sky; a procession of Barbarians, each in the costume of his country, passes across the wall; there are battles, in which elephants fight with men; an army besieges a great city, or rots to death in a defile between mountains; the ground is paved with dead men; crosses, each bearing its living burden, stand against the sky; a few figures of men and women appear again and again, expressing by their gestures the soul of the story.

Flaubert himself has pointed, with his unerring self-criticism, to the main defect of his book: "The pedestal is too large for the statue." There should have been, as he says, a hundred pages more about Salammbô. He declares: "There is not in my book an isolated or gratuitous description; all are useful to my characters, and have an influence, near or remote, on the action." This is true, and yet, all the same, the pedestal is too large for the statue. Salammbô, "always surrounded with grave and exquisite things," has something of the somnambulism which enters into the heroism of Judith; she has a hieratic beauty, and a consciousness as pale and vague as the moon whom she worships. She passes before us, "her body saturated with perfumes," encrusted with jewels like an idol, her head turreted with violet hair, the gold chain tinkling between her ankles; and is hardly more than an attitude, a fixed gesture, like the Eastern women whom one sees passing, with oblique eyes and mouths painted into smiles, their faces curiously traced into a work of art, in the languid movements of a pantomimic dance. The soul behind those eyes? the temperament under that at times almost terrifying mask? Salammbô is as inarticulate for us as the serpent, to whose drowsy beauty, capable of such sudden awakenings, hers seems half akin; they move before us in a kind of hieratic pantomime, a coloured, expressive thing, signifying nothing. Mâtho, maddened with love, "in an invincible stupor, like those who have drunk some draught of which they are to die," has the same somnambulistic life; the prey of Venus, he has an almost literal insanity, which, as Flaubert reminds us, is true to the ancient view of that passion. He is the only

quite vivid person in the book, and he lives with the intensity of a wild beast, a life "blinded alike" from every
inner and outer interruption to one or two fixed ideas.
The others have their places in the picture, fall into their
attitudes naturally, remain so many coloured outlines for
us. The illusion is perfect; these people may not be the
real people of history, but at least they have no self-con-
sciousness, no Christian tinge in their minds.

"The metaphors are few, the epithets definite," Flaubert tells us, of his style in this book, where, as he says,
he has sacrificed less "to the amplitude of the phrase and
to the period," than in *Madame Bovary*. The movement
here is in briefer steps, with a more earnest gravity, without any of the engaging weakness of adjectives. The style
is never archaic, it is absolutely simple, the precise word
being put always for the precise thing; but it obtains a
dignity, a historical remoteness, by the large seriousness
of its manner, the absence of modern ways of thought,
which, in *Madame Bovary*, bring with them an instinctively modern cadence.

Salammbô is written with the severity of history, but
Flaubert notes every detail visually, as a painter notes the
details of natural things. A slave is being flogged under
a tree: Flaubert notes the movement of the thong as
it flies, and tells us: "The thongs, as they whistled
through the air, sent the bark of the plane trees flying."
Before the battle of the Macar, the Barbarians are awaiting the approach of the Carthaginian army. First "the
Barbarians were surprised to see the ground undulate in
the distance." Clouds of dust rise and whirl over the
desert, through which are seen glimpses of horns, and, as
it seems, wings. Are they bulls or birds, or a mirage of
the desert? The Barbarians watch intently. "At last
they made out several transverse bars, bristling with uniform points. The bars became denser, larger; dark
mounds swayed from side to side; suddenly square bushes
came into view; they were elephants and lances. A single
shout, 'The Carthaginians!' arose." Observe how all that

is seen, as if the eyes, unaided by the intelligence, had found out everything for themselves, taking in one indication after another, instinctively. Flaubert puts himself in the place of his characters, not so much to think for them as to see for them.

Compare the style of Flaubert in each of his books, and you will find that each book has its own rhythm, perfectly appropriate to its subject-matter. The style, which has almost every merit and hardly a fault, becomes what it is by a process very different from that of most writers careful of form. Read Chateaubriand, Gautier, even Baudelaire, and you will find that the aim of these writers has been to construct a style which shall be adaptable to every occasion, but without structural change; the cadence is always the same. The most exquisite word-painting of Gautier can be translated rhythm for rhythm into English, without difficulty; once you have mastered the tune, you have merely to go on; every verse will be the same. But Flaubert is so difficult to translate because he has no fixed rhythm; his prose keeps step with no regular march-music. He invents the rhythm of every sentence, he changes his cadence with every mood or for the convenience of every fact. He has no theory of beauty in form apart from what it expresses. For him form is a living thing, the physical body of thought, which it clothes and interprets. "If I call stones blue, it is because blue is the precise word, believe me," he replies to Sainte-Beuve's criticism. Beauty comes into his words from the precision with which they express definite things, definite ideas, definite sensations. And in his book, where the material is so hard, apparently so unmalleable, it is a beauty of sheer exactitude which fills it from end to end, a beauty of measure and order, seen equally in the departure of the doves of Carthage at the time of their flight into Sicily, and in the lions feasting on the corpses of the Barbarians, in the defile between the mountains.

CHARLES BAUDELAIRE

BAUDELAIRE is little known and much misunderstood in England. Only one English writer has ever done him justice, or said anything adequate about him. As long ago as 1862 Swinburne introduced Baudelaire to English readers: in the columns of the *Spectator,* it is amusing to remember. In 1868 he added a few more words of just and subtle praise in his book on Blake, and in the same year wrote the magnificent elegy on his death, *Ave atque Vale.* There have been occasional outbreaks of irrelevant abuse or contempt, and the name of Baudelaire (generally misspelled) is the journalist's handiest brickbat for hurling at random in the name of respectability. Does all this mean that we are waking up, over here, to the consciousness of one of the great literary forces of the age, a force which has been felt in every other country but ours?

It would be a useful influence for us. Baudelaire desired perfection, and we have never realised that perfection is a thing to aim at. He only did what he could do supremely well, and he was in poverty all his life, not because he would not work, but because he would work only at certain things, the things which he could hope to do to his own satisfaction. Of the men of letters of our age he was the most scrupulous. He spent his whole life in writing one book of verse (out of which all French poetry has come since his time), one book of prose in which prose becomes a fine art, some criticism which is the sanest, subtlest, and surest which his generation produced, and a translation which is better than a marvellous original. What would French poetry be to-day if Baudelaire had never existed? As different a thing from what it is as English poetry would be without Rossetti. Neither of them is quite among the greatest poets, but they are more fascinating than the greatest, they influence more minds. And Baudelaire was an equally great critic. He discovered Poe, Wagner, and Manet. Where even Sainte-Beuve, with his vast materials, his vast general talent for criticism, went wrong in contemporary judgments, Baudelaire was infallibly right. He wrote neither verse nor prose with ease, but he would not permit himself to write either without inspiration. His work is without abundance, but it is without waste. It is made out of his whole intellect and all his nerves. Every poem is a train of thought and every essay is the record of sensation. This "romantic" had something classic in his moderation, a moderation which becomes at times as terrifying as Poe's logic. To "cultivate one's hysteria" so calmly, and to affront the reader (*Hypocrite lecteur, mon semblable, mon frère*) as a judge rather than as a penitent; to be a casuist in confession; to be so much a moralist, with so keen a sense of the ecstasy of evil: that has always bewildered the world, even in his own country, where the artist is allowed to live as experimentally as he writes. Baudelaire lived and died solitary, secret, a confessor of sins who has never told the whole truth, *le mauvais moine* of his own sonnet, an ascetic of passion, a hermit of the brothel.

To understand, not Baudelaire, but what we can of him, we must read, not only the four volumes of his collected works, but every document in Crépet's *Œuvres Posthumes,* and above all, the letters, and these have only now been collected into a volume, under the care of an editor who has done more for Baudelaire than any one since Crépet. Baudelaire put into his letters only what he cared to reveal of himself at a given moment: he has a different angle to distract the sight of every observer; and let no one think that he knows Baudelaire when he has read the letters to Poulet-Malassis, the friend and publisher, to whom he showed his business side, or the letters to la Présidente, the touchstone of his *spleen et idéal,* his chief experiment in the higher sentiments. Some of his carefully hidden virtues peep out at moments, it is true, but nothing that everybody has not long been aware of. We hear of his ill-luck with money, with proof-sheets, with his own health. The tragedy of the life which he chose, as he chose all things (poetry, Jeanne Duval, the "artificial paradises") deliberately, is made a little clearer to us; we can moralise over it if we like. But the man remains baffling, and will probably never be discovered.

As it is, much of the value of the book consists in those glimpses into his mind and intentions which he allowed people now and then to see. Writing to Sainte-Beuve, to Flaubert, to Soulary, he sometimes lets out, through mere sensitiveness to an intelligence capable of understanding him, some little interesting secret. Thus it is to Sainte-Beuve that he defines and explains the origin and real meaning of the *Petits Poèmes en Prose: Faire cent bagatelles laborieuses qui exigent une bonne humeur constante (bonne humeur nécessaire, même pour traiter des sujets tristes), une excitation bizarre qui a besoin de spectacles, de foules, de musiques, de réverbères même, voilà ce que j'ai voulu faire!* And, writing to some obscure person, he will take the trouble to be even more explicit, as in this symbol of the sonnet: *Avez-vous observé qu'un morceau de ciel aperçu par un soupirail, ou entre deux cheminées, deux rochers, ou par une arcade, donnait une idée plus profonde de l'infini que le grand panorama vu du haut d'une montagne?* It is to another casual person that he speaks out still more intimately (and the occasion of his writing is some thrill of gratitude towards one who had at last done "a little justice," not to himself, but to Manet): *Eh bien! on m'accuse, moi, d'imiter Edgar Poe! Savez-vous pourquoi j'ai si patiemment traduit Poe? Parce qu'il me resemblait. La première fois que j'ai ouvert un livre de lui, j'ai vu avec épouvante et ravissement, non seulement des sujets rêvés par moi, mais des phrases, pensées par moi, et écrites par lui, vingt ans auparavant.* It is in such glimpses as these that we see something of Baudelaire in his letters.

EDMOND AND JULES DE GONCOURT

MY FIRST visit to Edmond de Goncourt was in May, 1892. I remember my immense curiosity about that "House Beautiful," at Auteuil, of which I had heard so much, and my excitement as I rang the bell, and was shown at once into the garden, where Goncourt was just saying good-bye to some friends. He was carelessly dressed, without a collar, and with the usual loosely knotted large white scarf rolled round his neck. He was wearing a straw hat, and it was only afterwards that I could see the fine sweep of the white hair, falling across the forehead. I thought him the most distinguished-looking man of letters I had ever seen; for he had at once the distinction of race, of fine breeding, and of that delicate artistic genius which, with him, was so intimately a part of things beautiful and distinguished. He had the eyes of an old eagle; a general air of dignified collectedness; a rare, and a rarely charming, smile, which came out, like a ray of sunshine, in the instinctive pleasure of having said a witty or graceful thing to which one's response had been immediate. When he took me indoors, into that house which was a museum, I noticed the delicacy of his hands, and the tenderness with which he handled his treasures, touching them as if he loved them, with little, unconscious murmurs: *Quel goût! quel goût!* These rose-coloured rooms, with their embroidered ceilings, were filled with cabinets of beautiful things, Japanese carvings, and prints (the miraculous "Plongeuses"!), always in perfect condition (*Je cherche le beau*); albums had been made for him in Japan, and in these he inserted prints, mounting others upon silver and gold paper, which formed a sort of frame. He showed me his eighteenth-century designs, among which I remember his pointing out one (a Chardin, I think) as the first he had ever bought; he had been sixteen at the time, and he bought it for twelve francs.

When we came to the study, the room in which he worked, he showed me all of his own first editions, carefully bound, and first editions of Flaubert, Baudelaire, Gautier, with those, less interesting to me, of the men of later generations. He spoke of himself and his brother with a serene pride, which seemed to me perfectly dignified and appropriate; and I remember his speaking (with a parenthetic disdain of the *brouillard scandinave,* in which it seemed to him that France was trying to envelop herself; at the best it would be but *un mauvais brouillard*) of the endeavour which he and his brother had made to represent the only thing worth representing, *la vie vécue, la vraie vérité.* As in painting, he said, all depends on the way of seeing, *l'optique:* out of twenty-four men who will describe what they have all seen, it is only the twenty-fourth who will find the right way of expressing it. "There is a true thing I have said in my journal," he went on. "The thing is, to find a lorgnette" (and he put up his hands to his eyes, adjusting them carefully) "through which to see things. My brother and I invented a lorgnette, and the young men have taken it from us."

How true that is, and how significantly it states just what is most essential in the work of the Goncourts! It is a new way of seeing, literally a new way of seeing, which they have invented; and it is in the invention of this that they have invented that "new language" of which purists have so long, so vainly, and so thanklessly complained. You remember that saying of Masson, the mask of Gautier, in *Charles Demailly:* "I am a man for whom the visible world exists." Well, that is true, also, of the Goncourts; but in a different way.

"The delicacies of fine literature," that phrase of Pater always comes into my mind when I think of the Goncourts; and indeed Pater seems to me the only English writer who has ever handled language at all in their manner or spirit. I frequently heard Pater refer to certain of their books, to *Madame Gervaisais,* to *L'Art du*

XVIIIe Siècle, to *Chérie;* with a passing objection to what he called the "immodesty" of this last book, and a strong emphasis in the assertion that "that was how it seemed to him a book should be written." I repeated this once to Goncourt, trying to give him some idea of what Pater's work was like; and he lamented that his ignorance of English prevented him from what he instinctively realised would be so intimate an enjoyment. Pater was of course far more scrupulous, more limited, in his choice of epithet, less feverish in his variations of cadence; and naturally so, for he dealt with another subject-matter and was careful of another kind of truth. But with both there was that passionately intent preoccupation with "the delicacies of fine literature"; both achieved a style of the most personal sincerity: *tout grand écrivain de tous les temps,* said Goncourt, *ne se reconnaît absolument qu'à cela, c'est qu'il a une langue personnelle, une langue dont chaque page, chaque ligne, est signée, pour le lecteur lettré, comme si son nom était au bas de cette page, de cette ligne:* and this style, in both, was accused, by the "literary" criticism of its generation, of being insincere, artificial, and therefore reprehensible.

It is difficult, in speaking of Edmond de Goncourt, to avoid attributing to him the whole credit of the work which has so long borne his name alone. That is an error which he himself would never have pardoned. *Mon frère et moi* was the phrase constantly on his lips, and in his journal, his prefaces, he has done full justice to the vivid and admirable qualities of that talent which, all the same, would seem to have been the lesser, the more subservient, of the two. Jules, I think, had a more active sense of life, a more generally human curiosity; for the novels of Edmond, written since his brother's death, have, in even that excessively specialised world of their common observation, a yet more specialised choice and direction. But Edmond, there is no doubt, was in the strictest sense the writer; and it is above all for the qualities of its writing that the work of the Goncourts will live. It has

been largely concerned with truth—truth to the minute
details of human character, sensation, and circumstance,
and also of the document, the exact words, of the past;
but this devotion to fact, to the curiosities of fact, has
been united with an even more persistent devotion to the
curiosities of expression. They have invented a new
language: that was the old reproach against them; let it
be their distinction. Like all writers of an elaborate
carefulness, they have been accused of sacrificing both
truth and beauty to deliberate eccentricity. Deliberate
their style certainly was; eccentric it may, perhaps, sometimes have been; but deliberately eccentric, no. It was
their belief that a writer should have a personal style, a
style as peculiar to himself as his handwriting; and
indeed I seem to see in the handwriting of Edmond de
Goncourt just the characteristics of his style. Every
letter is formed carefully, separately, with a certain
elegant stiffness; it is beautiful, formal, too regular in the
"continual slight novelty" of its form to be quite clear
at a glance: very personal, very distinguished writing.

It may be asserted that the Goncourts are not merely
men of genius, but are perhaps the typical men of letters
of the close of our century. They have all the curiosities
and the acquirements, the new weaknesses and the new
powers, that belong to our age; and they sum up in
themselves certain theories, aspirations, ways of looking
at things, notions of literary duty and artistic conscience,
which have only lately become at all actual, and some of
which owe to them their very origin. To be not merely
novelists (inventing a new kind of novel), but historians;
not merely historians, but the historians of a particular
century, and of what was intimate and what is unknown
in it; to be also discriminating, indeed innovating critics of
art, but of a certain section of art, the eighteenth century,
in France and in Japan; to collect pictures and *bibelots,*
beautiful things, always of the French and Japanese
eighteenth century: these excursions in so many directions, with their audacities and their careful limitations,

their bold novelty and their scrupulous exactitude in detail, are characteristic of what is the finest in the modern conception of culture and the modern ideal in art. Look, for instance, at the Goncourts' view of history. *Quand les civilisations commencent, quand les peuples se forment, l'histoire est drame ou geste. . . . Les siècles qui ont précédé notre siècle ne demandaient à l'historien que le personnage de l'homme, et le portrait de son génie. . . . Le XIXᵉ siècle demande l'homme qui était cet homme d'État, cet homme de guerre, ce poète, ce peintre, ce grand homme de science ou de métier. L'âme qui était en cet acteur, le cœur qui a vécu derrière cet esprit, il les exige et les réclame; et s'il ne peut recueillir tout cet être moral, toute la vie intérieure, il commande du moins qu'on lui en apporte une trace, un jour, un lambeau, une relique.* From this theory, this conviction, came that marvellous series of studies in the eighteenth century in France (*La Femme au XVIIIᵉ Siècle, Portraits intimes du XVIIIᵉ Siècle, La du Barry,* and the others), made entirely out of documents, autograph letters, scraps of costume, engravings, songs, the unconscious self-revelations of the time, forming, as they justly say, *l'histoire intime; c'est ce roman vrai que la postérité appellera peut-être un jour l'histoire humaine.* To be the bookworm and the magician; to give the actual documents, but not to set barren fact by barren fact; to find a soul and a voice in documents, to make them more living and more charming than the charm of life itself: that is what the Goncourts have done. And it is through this conception of history that they have found their way to that new conception of the novel which has revolutionised the entire art of fiction.

Aujourd'hui, they wrote, in 1864, in the preface to *Germinie Lacerteux, que le Roman s'élargit et grandit, qu'il commence à être la grande forme sérieuse, passionnée, vivante, de l'étude littéraire et de l'enquête sociale, qu'il devient, par l'analyse et par la recherche psychologique, l'Histoire morale contemporaine, aujourd'hui*

que le Roman s'est imposé les devoirs de la science, il
peut en revendiquer les libertés et les franchises. Le
public aime les romans faux, is another brave declaration
in the same preface; *ce roman est un roman vrai.* But
what, precisely, is it that the Goncourts understood by
un roman vrai? The old notion of the novel was that it
should be an entertaining record of incidents or adventures told for their own sake; a plain, straightforward
narrative of facts, the aim being to produce as nearly as
possible an effect of continuity, of nothing having been
omitted, the statement, so to speak, of a witness on
oath; in a word, it is the same as the old notion of history,
drame ou geste. That is not how the Goncourts apprehend life, or how they conceive it should be rendered. As
in the study of history they seek mainly the *inédit,* caring
only to record that, so it is the *inédit* of life that they conceive to be the main concern, the real "inner history."
And for them the *inédit* of life consists in the noting of the
sensations; it is of the sensations that they have resolved
to be the historians; not of action, nor of emotion, properly speaking, nor of moral conceptions, but of an inner
life which is all made up of the perceptions of the senses.
It is scarcely too paradoxical to say that they are psy-
chologists for whom the soul does not exist. One thing,
they know, exists: the sensation flashed through the brain,
the image on the mental retina. Having found that, they
bodily omit all the rest as of no importance, trusting to
their instinct of selection, of retaining all that really
matters. It is the painter's method, a selection made
almost visually; the method of the painter who accumu-
lates detail on detail, in his patient, many-sided observation of his subject, and then omits everything which
is not an essential part of the *ensemble* which he sees.
Thus the new conception of what the real truth of things
consists in has brought with it, inevitably, an entirely new
form, a breaking up of the plain, straightforward narrative into chapters, which are generally quite disconnected, and sometimes of less than a page in length. A

very apt image of this new, curious manner of narrative has been found, somewhat maliciously, by M. Lemaître. *Un homme qui marche à l'intérieur d'une maison, si nous regardons du dehors, apparaît successivement à chaque fenêtre, et dans les intervalles nous échappe. Ces fenêtres, ce sont les chapitres de MM. de Goncourt. Encore,* he adds, *y a-t-il plusieurs de ces fenêtres où l'homme que nous attendions ne passe point.* That, certainly, is the danger of the method. No doubt the Goncourts, in their passion for the *inédit,* leave out certain things because they are obvious, even if they are obviously true and obviously important; that is the defect of their quality. To represent life by a series of moments, and to choose these moments for a certain subtlety and rarity in them, is to challenge grave perils. Nor are these the only perils which the Goncourts have constantly before them. There are others, essential to their natures, to their preferences. And, first of all, as we may see on every page of that miraculous *Journal,* which will remain, doubtless, the truest, deepest, most poignant piece of human history that they have ever written, they are sick men, seeing life through the medium of diseased nerves. *Notre œuvre entier,* writes Edmond de Goncourt, *repose sur la maladie nerveuse; les peintures de la maladie, nous les avons tirées de nous-mêmes, et, à force de nous disséquer, nous sommes arrivés à une sensitivité supra-aiguë que blessaient les infiniment petits de la vie.* This unhealthy sensitiveness explains much, the singular merits as well as certain shortcomings or deviations, in their work. The Goncourts' vision of reality might almost be called an exaggerated sense of the truth of things; such a sense as diseased nerves inflict upon one, sharpening the acuteness of every sensation; or somewhat such a sense as one derives from haschisch, which simply intensifies, yet in a veiled and fragrant way, the charm or the disagreeableness of outward things, the notion of time, the notion of space. What the Goncourts paint is the subtler poetry of reality, its unusual aspects, and they evoke it,

fleetingly, like Whistler; they do not render it in hard
outline, like Flaubert, like Manet. As in the world of
Whistler, so in the world of the Goncourts, we see cities
in which there are always fireworks at Cremorne, and
fair women reflected beautifully and curiously in mirrors.
It is a world which is extraordinarily real; but there is
choice, there is curiosity, in the aspect of reality which it
presents.

Compare the descriptions, which form so large a part
of the work of the Goncourts, with those of Théophile
Gautier, who may reasonably be said to have introduced
the practice of eloquent writing about places, and also
the exact description of them. Gautier describes miracu-
lously, but it is, after all, the ordinary observation carried to perfection, or, rather, the ordinary pictorial observation. The Goncourts only tell you the things that
Gautier leaves out; they find new, fantastic points of
view, discover secrets in things, curiosities of beauty,
often acute, distressing, in the aspects of quite ordinary
places. They see things as an artist, an ultra-subtle
artist of the impressionist kind, might see them; seeing
them indeed always very consciously with a deliberate
attempt upon them, in just that partial, selecting, creative way in which an artist looks at things for the purpose of painting a picture. In order to arrive at their
effects, they shrink from no sacrifice, from no excess;
slang, neologism, forced construction, archaism, barbarous epithet, nothing comes amiss to them, so long as it
tends to render a sensation. Their unique care is that the
phrase should live, should palpitate, should be alert,
exactly expressive, super-subtle in expression; and they
prefer indeed a certain perversity in their relations with
language, which they would have not merely a passionate
and sensuous thing, but complex with all the curiosities
of a delicately depraved instinct. It is the accusation of
the severer sort of French critics that the Goncourts have
invented a new language; that the language which they
use is no longer the calm and faultless French of the

**past. It is true; it is their distinction; it is the most
wonderful of all their inventions:** in order to render new
sensations, a new vision of things, they have invented a
new language.

LÉON CLADEL

I HOPE that the life of Léon Cladel by his daughter
Judith, which Lemerre has brought out in a pleasant
volume, will do something for the fame of one of the
most original writers of our time. Cladel had the good
fortune to be recognised in his lifetime by those whose
approval mattered most, beginning with Baudelaire, who
discovered him before he had printed his first book, and
helped to teach him the craft of letters. But so exceptional an artist could never be popular, though he
worked in living stuff and put the whole savour of his
countryside into his tragic and passionate stories. A
peasant, who writes about peasants and poor people, with
a curiosity of style which not only packs his vocabulary
with difficult words, old or local, and with unheard of
rhythms, chosen to give voice to some never yet articu-
lated emotion, but which drives him into oddities of
printing, of punctuation, of the very shape of his accents!
A page of Cladel has a certain visible uncouthness, and
at first this seems in keeping with his matter; but the
uncouthness, when you look into it, turns out to be
itself a refinement, and what has seemed a confused
whirl, an improvisation, to be the result really of
reiterated labour, whose whole aim has been to bring the
spontaneity of the first impulse back into the laboriously
finished work.

In this just, sensitive, and admirable book, written by
one who has inherited a not less passionate curiosity
about life, but with more patience in waiting upon it,
watching it, noting its surprises, we have a simple and
sufficient commentary upon the books and upon the

man. The narrative has warmth and reserve, and is at once tender and clear-sighted. *J'entrevois nettement,* she says with truth, *combien seront précieux pour les futurs historiens de la littérature du xixe siècle, les mémoires tracés au contact immédiat de l'artiste, exposés de ses faits et gestes particuliers, de ses origines, de la germination de ses croyances et de son talent; ses critiques à venir y trouveront de solides matériaux, ses admirateurs un aliment à leur piété et les philosophes un des aspects de l'Âme française.* The man is shown to us, *les élans de cette âme toujours grondante et fulgurante comme une forge, et les nuances de ce fiévreux visage d'apôtre, brun, fin et sinueux,* and we see the inevitable growth, out of the hard soil of Quercy and out of the fertilising contact of Paris and Baudelaire, of this whole literature, these books no less astonishing than their titles: *Ompdrailles-le-Tombeau-des-Lutteurs, Celui de la Croix-aux-Bœufs, La Fête Votive de Saint-Bartholomée-Porte-Glaive.* The very titles are an excitement. I can remember how mysterious and alluring they used to seem to me when I first saw them on the cover of what was perhaps his best book, *Les Va-Nu-Pieds.*

It is by one of the stories, and the shortest, in *Les Va-Nu-Pieds,* that I remember Cladel. I read it when I was a boy, and I cannot think of it now without a shiver. It is called *L'Hercule,* and it is about a Sandow of the streets, a professional strong man, who kills himself by an overstrain; it is not a story at all, it is the record of an incident, and there is only the strong man in it and his friend the zany, who makes the jokes while the strong man juggles with bars and cannon-balls. It is all told in a breath, without a pause, as if someone who had just seen it poured it out in a flood of hot words. Such vehemence, such pity, such a sense of the cruelty of the spectacle of a man driven to death like a beast, for a few pence and the pleasure of a few children; such an evocation of the sun and the streets and this sordid tragic thing happening to the sound of drum and cymbals;

such a vision in sunlight of a barbarous and ridiculous and horrible accident, lifted by the telling of it into a new and unforgettable beauty, I have never felt or seen in any other story of a like grotesque tragedy. It realises an ideal, it does for once what many artists have tried and failed to do; it wrings the last drop of agony out of that subject which it is so easy to make pathetic and effective. Dickens could not have done it, Bret Harte could not have done it, Kipling could not do it: Cladel did it only once, with this perfection.

Something like it he did over and over again, with unflagging vehemence, with splendid variations, in stories of peasants and wrestlers and thieves and prostitutes. They are all, as his daughter says, epic; she calls them Homeric, but there is none of the Homeric simplicity in this tumult of coloured and clotted speech, in which the language is tortured to make it speak. The comparison with Rabelais is nearer. *La recherche du terme vivant, sa mise en valeur et en saveur, la surabondance des vocables puisés à toutes sources . . . la condensation de l'action autour de ces quelques motifs éternels de l'épopée: combat, ripaille, palabre et luxure,* there, as she sees justly, are links with Rabelais. Goncourt, himself always aiming at an impossible closeness of written to spoken speech, noted with admiration *la vraie photographie de la parole avec ses tours, ses abréviations ses ellipses, son essoufflement presque.* Speech out of breath, that is what Cladel's is always; his words, never the likely ones, do not so much speak as cry, gesticulate, overtake one another. *L'âme de Léon Cladel,* says his daughter, *était dans un constant et flamboyant automme.* Something of the colour and fever of autumn is in all he wrote. Another writer since Cladel, who has probably never heard of him, has made heroes of peasants and vagabonds. But Maxim Gorki makes heroes of them, consciously, with a mental self-assertion, giving them ideas which he has found in Nietzsche. Cladel put into all his people some of his own passionate way of seeing "scarlet," to use Barbey d'Aurevilly's epithet: *un rural écarlate*. Vehement and voluminous, he overflowed: his whole aim as an artist, as a pupil of Baudelaire, was to concentrate, to hold himself back; and the effort added impetus to the checked overflow. To the realists he seemed merely extravagant; he saw certainly what they could not see; and his romance was always a fruit of the soil. The artist in him, seeming to be in conflict with the peasant, fortified, clarified the peasant, extracted from that hard soil a rare fruit. You see in his face an extraordinary mingling of the peasant, the visionary, and the dandy: the long hair and beard, the sensitive mouth and nose, the fierce brooding eyes, in which wildness and delicacy, strength and a kind of stealthiness, seem to be grafted on an inflexible peasant stock.

A NOTE ON ZOLA'S METHOD

THE art of Zola is based on certain theories, on a view of humanity which he has adopted as his formula. As a deduction from his formula, he takes many things in human nature for granted, he is content to observe at second-hand; and it is only when he comes to the filling-up of his outlines, the *mise-en-scène*, that his observation becomes personal, minute, and persistent. He has thus succeeded in being at once unreal where reality is most essential, and tediously real where a point-by-point reality is sometimes unimportant. The contradiction is an ingenious one, which it may be interesting to examine in a little detail, and from several points of view.

And, first of all, take *L'Assommoir*, no doubt the most characteristic of Zola's novels, and probably the best; and, leaving out for the present the broader question of his general conception of humanity, let us look at Zola's manner of dealing with his material, noting by the way certain differences between his manner and that of Goncourt, of Flaubert, with both of whom he has so often been compared, and with whom he wishes to challenge comparison. Contrast *L'Assommoir* with *Germinie Lacerteux,* which, it must be remembered, was written thirteen years earlier. Goncourt, as he incessantly reminds us, was the first novelist in France to deliberately study the life of the people, after precise documents; and *Germinie Lacerteux* has this distinction, among others, that it was a new thing. And it is done with admirable skill; as a piece of writing, as a work of art, it is far superior to Zola. But, certainly, Zola's work has a mass and bulk, a *fougue, a portée,* which Goncourt's lacks; and it has a savour of plebeian flesh which all the delicate art of Goncourt could not evoke. Zola sickens you with it; but there it is. As in all his books, but more than in most, there is something greasy, a smear of eating and drinking; the pages, to use his own phrase, *grasses des lichades du lundi.* In *Germinie Lacerteux* you never forget that Goncourt is an aristocrat; in *L'Assommoir* you never forget that Zola is a bourgeois. Whatever Goncourt touches becomes, by the mere magic of his touch, charming, a picture; Zola is totally destitute of charm. But how, in *L'Assommoir,* he drives home to you the horrid realities of these narrow, uncomfortable lives! Zola has made up his mind that he will say everything, without omitting a single item, whatever he has to say; thus, in *L'Assommoir,* there is a great feast which lasts for fifty pages, beginning with the picking of the goose, the day before, and going on to the picking of the goose's bones, by a stray marauding cat, the night after. And, in a sense, he does say everything; and there, certainly, is his novelty, his invention. He observes with immense persistence, but his observation, after all, is only that of the man in the street; it is simply carried into detail, deliberately. And, while Goncourt wanders away sometimes into arabesques, indulges in flourishes, so finely artistic is his sense of words and of the things they represent, so perfectly can he match a sensation or an impression by its figure in speech, Zola, on the contrary, never finds just the right word, and it is his persistent fumbling for it which produces these miles of description; four pages describing how two people went upstairs, from the ground floor to the sixth story, and then two pages afterwards to describe how they came downstairs again. Sometimes, by his prodigious diligence and minuteness, he succeeds in giving you the impression; often, indeed; but at the cost of what *ennui* to writer and reader alike! And so much of it all is purely unnecessary, has no interest in itself and no connection with the story: the precise details of Lorilleux's chain-making, bristling with technical terms: it was *la colonne* that he made, and only that particular kind of chain; Goujet's forge, and the machinery in the shed next door; and just how you cut out zinc with a large pair of scissors. When Goncourt gives you a long description of anything, even if you do not feel that it helps on the story very much, it is such a beautiful thing in itself, his mere way of writing it is so enchanting, that you find yourself wishing it longer, at its longest. But with Zola, there is no literary interests in the writing, apart from its clear and coherent expression of a given thing; and these interminable descriptions have no extraneous, or, if you will, implicit interest, to save them from the charge of irrelevancy; they sink by their own weight. Just as Zola's vision is the vision of the average man, so his vocabulary, with all its technicology, remains mediocre, incapable of expressing subtleties, incapable of a really artistic effect. To find out in a slang dictionary that a filthy idea can be expressed by an ingeniously filthy phrase in *argot*, and to use that phrase, is not a great feat, or, on purely artistic grounds, altogether desirable. To go to a chainmaker and learn the trade name of the various kinds of chain which he manufactures, and of the instruments with which he manufactures them, is not an elaborate process, or one which can be said to pay you for the little trouble which it no doubt takes. And it is not well to be too certain after all that Zola is always perfectly accurate in his use of all this manifold knowledge. The slang, for example; he went to books for it, in books he found it, and no one will ever find some of it but in books. However, my main contention is that Zola's general use of words is, to be quite frank, somewhat ineffectual. He tries to do what Flaubert did, without Flaubert's tools, and without the craftsman's hand at the back of the tools. His fingers are too thick; they leave a blurred line. If you want merely weight, a certain kind of force, you get it; but no more.

Where a large part of Zola's merit lies, in his persistent attention to detail, one finds also one of his chief defects. He cannot leave well alone; he cannot omit; he will not take the most obvious fact for granted. *Il marcha le premier, elle le suivit,* well, of course, she followed him, if he walked first: why mention the fact? That beginning of a sentence is absolutely typical; it is impossible for him to refer, for the twentieth time, to some unimportant character, without giving name and profession, not one or the other, but both, invariably both. He tells us particularly that a room is composed of four walls, that a table stands on its four legs. And he does not appear to see the difference between doing that and doing as Flaubert does, namely, selecting precisely the detail out of all others which renders or consorts with the scene in hand, and giving that detail with an ingenious exactness. Here, for instance, in *Madame Bovary,* is a characteristic detail in the manner of Flaubert: *Huit jours après, comme elle étendait du linge dans sa cour, elle fut prise d'un crachement de sang, et le lendemain, tandis que Charles avait le dos tourné pour fermer le rideau de la fenêtre, elle dit: "Ah! mon Dieu!" poussa un soupir et s'évanouit. Elle était morte.* Now that detail, brought in without the slightest emphasis, of the husband turning his back at the very instant that his wife dies, is a detail of immense psychological value; it indicates to us, at the very opening of the book, just the character of the man about whom

we are to read so much. Zola would have taken at least
two pages to say that, and, after all, he would not have
said it. He would have told you the position of the
chest of drawers in the room, what wood the chest of
drawers was made of, and if it had a little varnish
knocked off at the corner of the lower cornice, just where
it would naturally be in the way of people's feet as they
entered the door. He would have told you how Charles
leant against the other corner of the chest of drawers,
and that the edge of the upper cornice left a slight dent
in his black frock-coat, which remained visible half an
hour afterwards. But that one little detail, which Flaubert selects from among a thousand, that, no, he would
never have given us that!

And the language in which all this is written, apart
from the consideration of language as a medium, is really
not literature at all, in any strict sense. I am not, for the
moment, complaining of the colloquialism and the slang.
Zola has told us that he has, in *L'Assommoir,* used the
language of the people in order to render the people with
a closer truth. Whether he has done that or not is not
the question. The question is, that he does not give one
the sense of reading good literature, whether he speaks in
Delvau's *langue verte,* or according to the Academy's
latest edition of classical French. His sentences have no
rhythm; they give no pleasure to the ear; they carry no
sensation to the eye. You hear a sentence of Flaubert
and you see a sentence of Goncourt, like living things,
with forms and voices. But a page of Zola lies dull and
silent before you; it draws you by no charm, it has no
meaning until you have read the page that goes before
and the page that comes after. It is like cabinet-makers'
work, solid, well fitted together, and essentially made to
be used.

Yes, there is no doubt that Zola writes very badly,
worse than any other French writer of eminence. It is
true that Balzac, certainly one of the greatest, does, in a
sense, write badly; but his way of writing badly is very

different from Zola's, and leaves you with the sense of quite a different result. Balzac is too impatient with words; he cannot stay to get them all into proper order, to pick and choose among them. Night, the coffee, the wet towel, and the end of six hours' labour are often too much for him; and his manner of writing his novels on the proof-sheets, altering and expanding as fresh ideas came to him on each re-reading, was not a way of doing things which can possibly result in perfect writing. But Balzac sins from excess, from a feverish haste, the very extravagance of power; and, at all events, he "sins strongly." Zola sins meanly, he is penuriously careful, he does the best he possibly can; and he is not aware that his best does not answer all requirements. So long as writing is clear and not ungrammatical, it seems to him sufficient. He has not realised that without charm there can be no fine literature, as there can be no perfect flower without fragrance.

And it is here that I would complain, not as a matter of morals, but as a matter of art, of Zola's obsession by what is grossly, uninterestingly filthy. There is a certain simile in *L'Assommoir*, used in the most innocent connection, in connection with a bonnet, which seems to me the most abjectly dirty phrase which I have ever read. It is one thing to use dirty words to describe dirty things: that may be necessary, and thus unexceptionable. It is another thing again, and this, too, may well be defended on artistic grounds, to be ingeniously and wittily indecent. But I do not think a real man of letters could possibly have used such an expression as the one I am alluding to, or could so meanly succumb to certain kinds of prurience which we find in Zola's work. Such a scene as the one in which Gervaise comes home with Lantier, and finds her husband lying drunk asleep in his own vomit, might certainly be explained and even excused, though few more disagreeable things were ever written, on the ground of the psychological importance which it undoubtedly has, and the overwhelming way in which it drives home the point which it is the writer's business to make. But the worrying way in which *le derrière* and *le ventre* are constantly kept in view, without the slightest necessity, is quite another thing. I should not like to say how often the phrase "sa nudité de jolie fille" occurs in Zola. Zola's nudities always remind me of those which you can see in the *Foire au pain d'épice* at Vincennes, by paying a penny and looking through a peep-hole. In the laundry scenes, for instance in *L'Assommoir,* he is always reminding you that the laundresses have turned up their sleeves, or undone a button or two of their bodices. His eyes seem eternally fixed on the inch or two of bare flesh that can be seen; and he nudges your elbow at every moment, to make sure that you are looking too. Nothing may be more charming than a frankly sensuous description of things which appeal to the senses; but can one imagine anything less charming, less like art, than this prying eye glued to the peep-hole in the Gingerbread Fair?

Yet, whatever view may be taken of Zola's work in literature, there is no doubt that the life of Zola is a model lesson, and might profitably be told in one of Dr. Smiles's edifying biographies. It may even be brought as a reproach against the writer of these novels, in which there are so many offences against the respectable virtues, that he is too good a bourgeois, too much the incarnation of the respectable virtues, to be a man of genius. If the finest art comes of the intensest living, then Zola has never had even a chance of doing the greatest kind of work. It is his merit and his misfortune to have lived entirely in and for his books, with a heroic devotion to his ideal of literary duty which would merit every praise if we had to consider simply the moral side of the question. So many pages of copy a day, so many hours of study given to mysticism, or Les Halles; Zola has always had his day's work marked out before him, and he has never swerved from it. A recent life of Zola tells us something about his way of getting up a subject. "Immense preparation had been necessary for the *Faute de l'Abbé Mouret*. Mountains of note-books were heaped up on his table, and for months Zola was plunged in the study of religious works. All the mystical part of the book, and notably the passages having reference to the cultus of Mary, was taken from the works of the Spanish Jesuits. The *Imitation of Jesus Christ* was largely drawn upon, many passages being copied almost word for word into the novel—much as in *Clarissa Harlowe,* that other great realist, Richardson, copied whole passages from the Psalms. The description of life in a grand seminary was given him by a priest who had been dismissed from ecclesiastical service. The little church of Sainte Marie des Batignolles was regularly visited."

How commendable all that is, but, surely, how futile! Can one conceive of a more hopeless, a more ridiculous task, than that of setting to work on a novel of ecclesiastical life as if one were cramming for an examination in religious knowledge? Zola apparently imagines that he can master mysticism in a fortnight, as he masters the police regulations of Les Halles. It must be admitted that he does wonders with his second-hand information, alike in regard to mysticism and Les Halles. But he succeeds only to a certain point, and that point lies on the nearer side of what is really meant by success. Is not Zola himself, at his moments, aware of this? A letter written in 1881, and printed in Mr. Sherard's life of Zola, from which I have just quoted, seems to me very significant.

"I continue to work in a good state of mental equilibrium. My novel (*Pot-Bouille*) is certainly only a task requiring precision and clearness. No *bravoura,* not the least lyrical treat. It does not give me any warm satisfaction, but it amuses me like a piece of mechanism with a thousand wheels, of which it is my duty to regulate the movements with the most minute care. I ask myself the question: Is it good policy, when one feels that one has passion in one, to check it, or even to bridle it? If one of my books is destined to become immortal, it will, I am sure, be the most passionate one."

Est-elle en marbre ou non, la Vénus de Milo? said the Parnassians, priding themselves on their muse with her *peplum bien sculpté.* Zola will describe to you the exact shape and the exact smell of the rags of his naturalistic muse; but has she, under the tatters, really a human heart? In the whole of Zola's works, amid all his exact and impressive descriptions of misery, all his endless annals of the poor, I know only one episode which brings tears to the eyes, the episode of the child-martyr Lalie in *L'Assommoir.* "A piece of mechanism with a thousand wheels," that is indeed the image of this immense and wonderful study of human life, evolved out of the brain of a solitary student who knows life only by the report of his documents, his friends, and, above all, his formula.

Zola has defined art, very aptly, as nature seen through a temperament. The art of Zola is nature seen through a formula. This professed realist is a man of theories who studies life with a conviction that he will find there such and such things which he has read about in scientific books. He observes, indeed, with astonishing minuteness, but he observes in support of preconceived ideas. And so powerful is his imagination that he has created a whole world which has no existence anywhere but in his own brain, and he has placed there imaginary beings, so much more logical than life, in the midst of surroundings which are themselves so real as to lend almost a semblance of reality to the embodied formulas who inhabit them.

It is the boast of Zola that he has taken up art at the point where Flaubert left it, and that he has developed that art in its logical sequence. But the art of Flaubert, itself a development from Balzac, had carried realism, if not in *Madame Bovary,* at all events in *L'Éducation Sentimentale,* as far as realism can well go without ceasing to be art. In the grey and somewhat sordid history of Frédéric Moreau there is not a touch of romanticism, not so much as a concession to style, a momentary escape of the imprisoned lyrical tendency. Everything is observed, everything is taken straight from life: realism sincere, direct, implacable, reigns from end to end of the book. But with what consummate art all this mass of observation is disintegrated, arranged, composed! with what infinite delicacy it is manipulated in the service of an unerring sense of construction! And Flaubert has no theory, has no prejudices, has only a certain impatience with human imbecility. Zola, too, gathers his documents, heaps up his mass of observation, and then, in this unhappy "development" of the principles of art which produced *L'Éducation Sentimentale,* flings everything pell-mell into one overflowing *pot-au-feu.* The probabilities of nature and the delicacies of art are alike drowned beneath a flood of turbid observation, and in the end one does not even feel convinced that Zola really knows his subject. I remember once hearing M. Huysmans, with his look and tone of subtle, ironical malice, describe how Zola, when he was writing *La Terre,* took a drive into the country in a victoria, to see the peasants. The English papers once reported an interview in which the author of *Nana,* indiscreetly questioned as to the amount of personal observation he had put into the book, replied that he had lunched with an actress of the Variétés. The reply was generally taken for a joke, but the lunch was a reality, and it was assuredly a rare experience in the life of solitary diligence to which we owe so many impersonal studies in life. Nor did Zola, as he sat silent by the side of Mlle. X., seem to be making much use of the opportunity. The language of the miners in *Germinal,* how much of local colour is there in that? The interminable additions and divisions, the extracts from a financial gazette, in *L'Argent,* how much of the real temper and idiosyncrasy of the financier do they give us? In his description of places, in his *mise-en-scène,* Zola puts down what he sees with his own eyes, and, though it is often done at utterly dispro-

portionate length, it is at all events done with exactitude.
But in the far more important observation of men and
women, he is content with second-hand knowledge, the
knowledge of a man who sees the world through a
formula. Zola sees in humanity *la bête humaine*. He sees
the beast in all its transformations, but he sees only the
beast. He has never looked at life impartially, he has
never seen it as it is. His realism is a distorted idealism,
and the man who considers himself the first to paint
humanity as it really is will be remembered in the future
as the most idealistic writer of his time.